# SWING

## Also available from Infamous Books

*The White House*
by JaQuavis Coleman

*Black Lotus*
by K'wan

*H.N.I.C.*
by Albert "Prodigy" Johnson with Steven Savile

*Ritual*
by Albert "Prodigy" Johnson and Steven Savile
(forthcoming)

# CHAPTER 1

# No Sins As Long As There's Permission

## **Tori & Kevin**

THE WAY HIS SHAFT WAS RUBBING AGAINST MY CLITORIS gave me a feeling I had never had during sex before. He rotated his pelvis like he was dancing to a reggae song, with a little force and a whole lot of passion. It felt entirely too good.

Meanwhile, the other he was getting his dick sucked. I watched out the corner of my eye. Yes, there were two he's in the room. One he was penetrating me and the other was my husband, Kevin.

This was Kevin and my first trip to Puss & Boots, an exclusive swingers club in Atlanta. It was a surprise for Kevin's thirtieth birthday. I blindfolded him and we jumped in the back of a town car. I walked him inside the club and didn't remove his blindfold until we were smack dead in the middle of the dance floor surrounded by nudity and sexual acts. He was pleasantly surprised. His dick got hard in point two seconds. We were already drunk from the rounds of Amsterdam we had consumed earlier at Cheetah's, a strip club we frequented.

Our being intoxicated—mixed with the excitement of all that was happening around us—removed any reservations. Kevin laid me down right there on the dance floor. He pulled his dick through the zipper of his jeans and lifted my dress. I wasn't wearing any panties—I never did when Kevin and I went to Cheetah's. I don't think I need to explain.

He inserted his horny, erect dick into me. And we had sex right there between two women dancing with each other and a couple sipping drinks talking about who they wanted to fuck that night. We didn't care if anyone was watching us. In fact, we hoped people were watching. It added to the pleasure.

We ended up only fucking each other once, although we did interact with other couples, Kevin fondling a titty here, me jerking a dick there. It was fun. Exciting. Gave our new marriage the spark I thought it needed.

I know what you're thinking. Why would a *new* marriage need spark? Well, here's the thing: Kevin and I may have only been married a year but we'd been together for ten. We met in college. I was a freshman, he, a junior. We started dating immediately. We've been inseparable since. So my entire college experience was null and void. No parties, no hangovers, no one-night stands. I was a girlfriend the whole time. Don't get me wrong, I enjoyed it. I loved Kevin. He loved me, deeply. We had our own fun together, and I didn't feel like I was missing out on anything at the time. But now I was pushing thirty. Already married. Having kids was a daily discussion in our household, mainly brought up by Kevin. I felt like any chances of me experimenting with my wilder side were soon to be over. And I was afraid of that. I wished I had just gotten it all out of my system in college. But Kevin came too soon. No pun intended. So there I was, trying to inject all that I had missed out on into our marriage. He was going along with it too. And what man wouldn't?

The circular movement increased in speed. My clitoris was dancing with joy. My senses heightened. I could hear my heartbeat racing through my chest. My body jerked. For a millisecond I was scared. But the wave of vibrations that came next, starting from my head and ending in my toes, transformed fear into an emotion I couldn't yet identify. I blurted out some words, or should I say sounds. My thighs shook. Then there was this release. I felt completely at ease. This was a first for me, and by the look on his face, it was a first for him too.

In ten years of being with Kevin, I had never had an orgasm. But after only twenty-two minutes, I was experiencing my very first one with a guy I was meeting for the first time. A tear rolled out from the corner of my eye. It slid backward toward my ear. I hoped Kevin didn't see it. The room was pretty dim so maybe not. I didn't want to wipe it and bring attention to it, so I left it to evaporate. Maybe it would disguise itself as sweat.

I couldn't seem to turn my head away from him. Even though I wanted bad to look over at my husband, assure him I was still his. But I was paralyzed. Or maybe just my eyes were. Fixated on his. Apparently his had the same paralysis. Our gaze was unbreakable. I could only imagine how Kevin was feeling. If it were me, I'd be a disaster. I'd probably throw a temper tantrum. It would definitely be time to go. I was waiting for the tug, but an abrupt laughter broke out instead. From her.

It dislocated our gaze, which I was sure was its purpose. I looked over at Kevin while the other he carefully slid out of me. Well, maybe he wasn't being careful. It felt more like reluctance. I smiled at Kevin, hoping he couldn't tell it was forced. He grinned. Or maybe grimaced. It was dark.

I sat up slowly, taking time to glance over at his wife. Her laugh was just tapering off. I gave her a fake smile too—well, an uncomfortable smile.

She returned it as she patted her husband's butt. "He's great, isn't he?" These were the first words I heard after my first climax. I would always remember them.

Kevin was watching me closely. I could feel his eyes.

He was waiting for me to say the wrong thing. I wasn't going to answer. I was sure the question was rhetorical anyway. As if the orgasm didn't tell it all. No need to fan the flames.

"You think we should exchange numbers?" he asked, pulling his black boxer briefs over his perfectly sculpted pelvis. He could have been an underwear model—he was a hell of a specimen. His honey-toned skin was so smooth it looked like it was painted onto his muscular arms and brick-like abs. He was hairless. No tattoos. His features were pronounced: dark eyebrows that appeared naturally arched, tiny light brown eyes the same color as his skin, well-defined cheekbones, a thin pointed nose, and crescent-shaped lips that had some plump to them. They gave me all sorts of ideas.

"We'll see each other again," his wife said, nodding at Kevin and me. Her eyes were low, though, almost closed. She wasn't being sincere. I couldn't blame her. It was obvious her husband had never brought her to the place he had gotten me to.

Kevin didn't respond. He was in the same boat as her, I guessed. I was sure he'd prefer it if this was the last time we saw each other. He looked at me. "Tori?"

I played along with her. "Sure we will."

"Well that was fun," she concluded, standing up, a white towel covering only the bottom half of her nude body. She was a white woman, but tanned to perfection. Her makeup was flawless. She wore her blond hair straight down her back. It was clear she worked out too. That was one thing the two had in common: she was in as good as shape as he was. I must say, she looked great for an older woman. Not that she had revealed her age to us, but I was privy to knowledge that she was a cougar—a sugar mama, actually. Their relationship appeared more like mother/son than husband/wife.

She grabbed his hand, and before the *goodbye* that was sitting on his lips could jump off, she squeezed it. I didn't see her do it, but I caught his reaction and he didn't say goodbye. Thinking back, that is another thing I regret about that night. Maybe had he said those words, it would have been the end of it. Maybe it *would* have been the last time we saw each other.

Kevin gathered our towels, handing me mine. I used the tip to wipe away my bodily fluids. While I felt around for my shoes, he finally spoke his mind.

"What the hell happened?"

I landed on one shoe and slid my foot in. "What do you mean?"

"Did he . . . did you . . . ?"

I put my hand up to my husband's face, palming the right side. He was no underwear-model prototype, but he was mine. His average build and common features were what I loved about him. I looked him in his eyes. "It doesn't even matter. This is all about you tonight. Did you enjoy yourself?"

He moved my hand from his face, nodded his head, and mumbled, "It was cool." Yet his entire demeanor told a different story.

"Baby, I did this for you," I whined. "I worked on this surprise for months, please don't let it end like this."

I wanted him to walk out of the club with the same excitement and thrill that he felt when he'd walked in and I removed his blindfold.

"It's cool. Let's go."

"No, it's not." I understood how he felt. Like I said, if the shoe were on the other foot—well, in this case, if the condom was on the other dick—I would have been feeling some type of way too. But I didn't want that for him. It was his birthday. His thirtieth at that. A trip to a swingers club was supposed to have been the surprise of a lifetime.

In my heels I came to his chin. I started kissing him on his neck, chin, and bottom lip. I wrapped my arms around his neck. I imagined it was he who had made me reach my peak. My energy began to transfer to him and his guard slowly receded.

"You are the only man I want and need. Don't you ever forget that. What we did tonight was a milestone in our relationship. Something for the books. And as long as it's a *we* thing, it shouldn't be a bad thing."

His arms found their way around my waist, hands crossed on my butt. I had reclaimed him.

"You're right," he said. "As long as we only do it together. All or none."

"And as long as at the end of the day, we know who we each belong to," I added.

And with that we sealed an allegiance. No signatures, just our words and our hearts—ironically, two of mankind's most susceptible, breakable elements. Truth was, neither one of us knew what we had gotten ourselves into. Yet somehow we thought we'd mastered it.

## Danielle & Stewart

As Stewart pulled into the parking lot, I slid a Molly under my tongue and took a swig of the Deer Park water I had in the cup holder. I adjusted the pasties on my pink nipples, then pulled close my chinchilla to cover my breasts. As I stepped out of the passenger seat of our latest purchase, my coat brushed the concrete. I felt so damn sexy.

"Welcome back, Mrs. Oxford," said the valet who rushed to my door the moment we pulled the Lotus into the lot.

"Thank you, honey," I purred at the young guy.

On the other side of the car stood Stewart, my tall, husky, handsomely bald husband. Everybody thought he was an athlete. We let them believe that. Our lifestyle supported the theory and it was better than telling them what we really did for a living.

Stewart peeled a hundred-dollar bill from a wad that rested atop the stack of flyers he had in his hand for our annual Christmas party. He gave the bill to the valet— the very reason it nearly became a relay race between the attendants every time we pulled up. It was like seeing Ed McMahon coming: payday.

"You know what to do with it," he told the guy.

The valet looked at the bill before folding it in his hand and nodding. "Thank you, sir." He took Stewart's place in the driver's seat.

Trying to steal one last glimpse of myself in the car's chrome body, I caught the reflection of the club's neon *Puss & Boots* sign. And boy did I feel at home.

An overdressed Stewart, in his blazer, V-neck, jeans, and loafers, used the hand that wasn't stuffed with flyers to open the club's door for me. He was such a gentleman. Upon entering, we were greeted by Kelsey, a beautiful, tall, slender, tanned brunette. She could've easily been a Kardashian, down to the K name. The only thing she was missing was a lot of ass. She had a little bump but nothing that could stand beside that Kardashian clan.

Anyway, she was the manager, and to prove that point she wore a tie on top of her bra, and instead of just panties or a thong like the other female employees wore, she opted for a miniskirt. Or the occasional pair of booty shorts.

"Mr. and Mrs. Oxford," Kelsey smiled, reaching her hand out to accept my fur as Stewart stripped it off my back. "Looking stunning as usual," she said to my nakedness.

"Thank you, darling," I ate it right up. I loved compliments.

"Did Sofia clean our room?" Stewart asked Kelsey's back as she walked toward the office carrying my coat.

"She sure did," Kelsey called from inside the office, then returned with a key which she placed in Stewart's palm. "She left about a half hour ago. Said she locked up."

Sofia was our housekeeper and the only person we trusted to clean our room at Puss & Boots.

"Is Lyssa here?" I asked Kelsey. "Her tongue and my pussy have a lunch date."

Stewart smirked and shook his head. "Danielle won the costume contest last month," he explained.

"I remember," Kelsey grinned. "And she's been try-ing to get you to her house ever since. You know, she and Jake are very strict about doing anything here. They don't like mixing business and pleasure."

"I'll do her one better," I said as I reached over and grabbed the stack of flyers from my husband's grip. I passed one to Kelsey. "She can come to our house. We're having our annual Christmas party . . ." Handing the flyers back to my husband I added, "You tell her she has no more excuses."

Kelsey glanced over the flyer and nodded.

I cupped my breasts and mashed them together. "You ready?" I looked at my husband.

He extended his free hand. "After you."

We opened the door that separated the real world from our fantasy and I strutted through. There were nude bodies everywhere: on the dance floor under strobe lights, at the bar carrying on casual conversations, in the dining area soaking up alcohol with food from the buffet, in the Jacuzzi, the pool, around the billiards table, scattered on leather couches and oversized daybeds. It was like the Garden of Eden, except Adam and Eve were multiplied by about fifty and that serpent that we know as temptation was the life of the party.

"A Cîroc Coconut," I told Nina, one of the scantily clad bartenders who stopped what she was doing to come over and take our drink order.

A cute couple at the bar who had witnessed the

special service looked our way. They had to be wondering who we were to deserve it. *Game time*, I thought, and I took that opportunity to introduce myself. It was ritual.

"I love your breasts," I complimented the golden-complexioned woman. *Flatter first. Then probe.* "Did you get those done here in Atlanta?"

The woman smiled bashfully. She was a newcomer. Great.

"Thank you," she said. "Texas."

Just what I wanted to hear. She was an out-of-towner. Stewart and I preferred out-of-towners. That way, the chances of us ever seeing them again were slim to none. I had to be certain, though, so I hit her with a follow-up question.

"Are you visiting? Or are you like most Atlantans and you migrated here?" By now, my drink was in front of me. I grabbed it and sipped.

"Visiting," the woman replied, still smiling. Then she looked over her shoulder at the pale-skinned, light-haired, thin guy she was with. Perhaps she felt like he was being left out.

That was Stewart's cue. And he took it. His hand extended to the guy, he said, "How you doin', man? I'm Stew."

The guy let go of his cup, shook his hand a little to

rid his palm of moisture, and received Stewart's hand-shake. "Brent," he said.

We women followed suit.

"I'm Victoria." She placed her hand on those titties I liked so much.

"And I'm—"

"Danielle," Victoria beat me to the end of my sentence. "I heard the bartender say, *Here comes Danielle.*"

"Oh you did, did you?" Then I paused my conversation with Victoria. "Aye, Nina!" I projected over the music and chatter.

She darted my way. "Another one, Mrs. Oxford?"

I leaned in, my ear as close to her mouth as the counter between us would allow. "*Mrs. Oxford*, you say?" I winked at Victoria. She couldn't help but chuckle.

"Yes," Nina answered matter-of-factly.

"Oh, okay." I straightened back up. "Just was making sure you knew the correct way to address me."

"Of course." Nina put on a chipper smile, then shot a quick, cold glance at Victoria and Brent.

I loved power as much as I did compliments. And from the looks on Brent's and Victoria's faces, they loved that I had it. They were hooked. Now I just had to reel them in.

"Good," I said to Nina. "Now, could you get that sexy gentleman over there," I motioned toward Brent, "another one of whatever he was drinking?"

"Sure thing," she replied, scurrying to fulfill my request.

Then I got back to business. "Well, now that the introductions are out of the way, would you two like to see our room?"

Victoria's smile widened along with her glassy eyes. "Your room?"

"In case you haven't noticed, we're not typical customers. We have a pretty unique relationship with the owners." I sipped my drink.

"We've noticed," Brent chimed in.

*Make them feel like tonight is their lucky night.* "So it looks like you two have a bit of beginner's luck. First time here, visiting from Texas, and you stumble upon the VIP couple with their own room," I smiled. *Now go in for the kill.* I took the pineapple slice off my cup and, looking Victoria deep in her hazel eyes, stuck my tongue through the small gap in the center of it. I slowly moved my tongue up and down. Either the Molly had kicked in or I was becoming a better actress by the minute. Whatever the case, I got her.

"I'd like to see your room," Victoria said in a sexy little whisper. Then she gazed over her shoulder at Brent again.

He shrugged.

"It's laid out too," Stewart assured.

Victoria got up from her barstool and she and Brent fell in line behind Stewart and me, off to our VIP room. *One couple down.*

In the hallway where our room was, there were six private rooms total. And I don't mean private in the sense of belonging to one particular couple like ours belonged exclusively to us. I mean they had doors that could be closed and locked, whereas the other rooms and areas in the back of the club were open for all to see and congregate. Those areas were usually packed with people having orgies. Basically, whoever was in close proximity to you and your mate was whom you ended up swapping with. And it usually happened without much talk or thought. Like one minute you would be giving your man head and the next some random girl was sharing the task with you. Then you'd feel someone fingering you while someone else was rubbing your breasts. And before you knew it, you were engaged in all kinds of sex with all kinds of people. It was fun in our younger days when we were wild and free. But now we did what we did because it actually served a purpose in our lives. I mean, the selection process and the privacy were great, but we did it this way for the end goal—the bigger picture.

On the way to our room, some familiar faces greeted us. Others just stared. They seemed to think we owned the place. Why else could Stewart be fully dressed in the section of the club where signs clearly stated, *No Clothes Permitted Beyond this Point*? My answer would be, if anyone ever asked, *We paid the price*. I laughed at my own thoughts. But it was fact. Stewart and I paid close to ten grand to renovate our room to our liking, plus we paid twice the yearly membership fee everyone else did. So we could do what we pleased.

We were like celebrities at Puss & Boots, and the couple tailing us were groupies who had lucked out and been chosen from the crowd. I laughed at myself again. No one noticed though. Everybody was back to moaning and groaning. Licking and sticking. I loved it too. This was my scene.

We approached our door. Stewart dug in his jeans pocket and pulled out a key, the one Kelsey had given him. He put it back and retrieved a different one, which he used to unlock the door.

Inside the room, Victoria and Brent really opened up. It could've been the room itself: the leather walls, mirrored mosaic ceilings, plush custom bed, and flat screen looping our favorite porn flicks. Or the fact that they had both finished their drinks. The privacy might have been a factor too. It all worked in our favor.

Without any instruction or guidance, Victoria started undressing Stewart. Brent, watching his naked woman position herself to go down on another man, began lightly stroking his white dick. I decided to match Victoria and give her man the same pleasure she was now giving mine.

We were both on our knees, pulling dicks in and out of our mouths, and I felt myself getting wetter and wetter. I initiated our move from the middle of the floor to the circular rotating bed. That was our main attraction. That and the swing.

I laid on my back, bringing Brent's dick to my face. I felt my legs being parted. And from under Brent's balls I could see a head full of long silky black hair moving down between my thighs. My husband was bald, so go figure.

Victoria licked away at my clitoris while Stewart seized the opportunity to penetrate her from the back. Of course, he put on a condom first. That was our one rule.

She squealed at first, surprised by his size. "Is that thing real?"

I caressed her shoulders and told my husband to take it easy. What she was doing to me was too good to be interrupted by every painful stroke.

He slowed his tempo, which made the whole show that much better. His facial expressions were priceless. The amount of pleasure he had to be feeling to make those faces aroused me even more.

I turned my attention back to the head of hair between my legs. I rubbed my fingers through it, and on occasion I would palm the head to keep it right in a particular spot. Simultaneously I would push my hips forward as if I were riding her tongue. It created a nice juicy pressure against my clit. It made me gasp. And whenever I did, it allowed her guy's dick to coast deeper down my throat. And he was taking full advantage of those moments. A few times, causing me to gag. But it was the nature of having sex in a group. Everyone wanted to seize every opportunity to be pleased beyond his or her wildest dreams.

As he pumped, she licked, and I sucked, it was like an assembly line. We switched positions numerous times before all of us had orgasms—the men cumming twice apiece. It was spectacular. More than I expected from the seemingly shy couple from Texas.

At the end, I stretched out on the bed and just smiled. My whole body felt jubilant.

"You guys smoke?" Stewart asked, from his seat on the edge of the bed.

Victoria smiled her answer. Brent said, "It's been awhile, but what the hell . . ."

Stewart stood up, picked his jeans up off the floor, and slipped them on. Then he walked over to our stash spot behind the TV screen. He pulled out the rolling papers, the marijuana, and the lighter. I just watched him, admiring his sex appeal. It amazed me that after eight years together and six married, I was still mesmerized by his every movement.

Victoria and Brent wrapped their *Puss & Boots*– stamped white towels around their waists. Stewart prepared our session. In the next couple hours, Stewart and I would smoke, eat, fill up on more drinks, and do it all over again with another unsuspecting couple. It was all ritual. Thursday through Sunday, ten p.m. till three, maybe four a.m., ongoing until we pressed *Stop Record* on the hidden camera in our VIP room. It was genius.

## JuJu & Ferrari

Getting back into their clothes in the locker room, JuJu and Ferrari exchanged not one word. Their silence left them to their thoughts. His—of that moment and how fucking magical it had been. The power he had over a human body. The earthquake that erupted in her flesh. How her mouth opened to scream but she could barely produce a whisper. The tear. He did that. And he felt proud. It gave him a cheerfulness he couldn't mask, no matter how hard he tried.

JuJu's thoughts paralleled Ferrari's but the feeling

she got when she replayed the moment was far different. There was no sense of pride. She was envious. This fresh-faced first-timer got to experience something with her husband that she had been trying to achieve for years. The reason she introduced the idea of occasional visits to a swingers club in the first place was to find somebody who could give her an orgasm.

"JuJu, Ferrari!" a voice squealed.

The couple looked around the corner and located the face.

"Danielle and Stew," JuJu smiled.

"It's been a long time." Danielle caressed Ferrari's pecs. "What occasion brings you two here tonight?"

"We're celebrating five years today," JuJu answered.

"Congratulations," Stew said, holding up his Heineken bottle.

"Thanks, man," Ferrari said.

"Why are you leaving already?" Danielle asked. "I wanna give you two an anniversary present." She fell to her knees and immediately started motor-boating Ferrari's package.

The group laughed as she stood back up.

"You know, I've been dying to do that," Danielle slurred.

"One day," JuJu said. "We have an early flight tomorrow."

"Where are you guys going?" Stewart asked.

"Tahiti," JuJu answered. "I got us a nice bungalow over the water. We're gonna rekindle our romance."

"Sweet," Stewart said, nodding his head.

Danielle reached out and gently squeezed both of JuJu's breasts. "Well, if y'all want some company, Stew and I can fly out there in a couple days." She winked at Ferrari while still having her way with his wife's breasts.

"Excuse my wife," Stewart interjected, "she's a ball of sex drive."

"It's cool," Ferrari said, a slight smile on his face. "Next time we come we have to . . ."

"Yes, definitely," JuJu cosigned. "Next time." She kissed Danielle on her lips and then gently removed her hands from her breasts. "Can't you see this girl's in heat, Stew? Go get her some dick . . . or some pussy."

They all laughed again.

"Yeah, I better before she rapes one of you," Stew added to the comedy.

Moments later, JuJu and Ferrari were completely dressed and ready to leave the locker room.

"Well, it was good seeing you," JuJu said as she headed to the door.

"Oh, wait," Danielle stopped the couple. "Honey, give them a flyer."

"Oh yeah, of course." Stewart dug in his back pocket. He pulled out a flyer and handed it to Ferrari. "We're having our annual Christmas party."

"Come out," Danielle encouraged, "we're going to have live shows, contests, the works. If you leave without having an orgasm you can sue us for all we got." She giggled.

The word *orgasm* caught their attention. JuJu was thinking that the Christmas party might give her what she had been so desperately looking for. Ferrari was thinking that perhaps he could recapture the experience he'd had that night. It was his first time making a woman cum, and he didn't want it to be his last.

"We'll be there," JuJu said.

"Yeah, for sure," Ferrari agreed.

"Great," Danielle said, kissing each of them on their lips one last time.

"Y'all enjoy your trip," Stewart said as the couple walked out of the locker room.

"Thanks!" JuJu yelled back. Ferrari waved goodbye.

Outside, the cold air was a major contrast to the steamy humidity of Puss & Boots. JuJu gave the valet her ticket and he fled to get the couple's vehicle.

"Is everything all right?" Ferrari asked his wife while they waited for their car to pull up.

"Yes, why do you ask?"

"You told Danielle and Stew we were going to Tahiti tomorrow."

"Everything's fine," JuJu said with a roll of her eyes.

"Why did you tell them that?"

JuJu's eyes suddenly squinted with fury, her lips tightened. "Because I did. Why are you questioning me?"

Their car arrived. In a snap JuJu put on a smile and tipped the valet. She hurried into the driver's seat, while Ferrari reluctantly got in the other side. Their ride home was as silent as their locker room experience before Danielle and Stewart had breathed life into it.

Ferrari took the opportunity to pretend to fall asleep. His mind, though, was spinning. He couldn't believe he had finally met his infatuation in person and had the chance to make love to her—something he had dreamed about for almost a year. Ever since he had seen those words on her Facebook page: *One is not wealthy until he has things money cannot buy.* He had simply written under it, *This couldn't be more true.* And that had sparked a cyber affair he never saw coming. Over the ensuing months, he told himself numerous times he would end it, usually after JuJu discovered a message or two and threatened him. But he couldn't help himself. Despite all the number changes, deleted online accounts, and spying by JuJu, he always managed to find his way back to his computer love. And tonight was his dream manifested.

The rumbling of the garage door pulled the plug on Ferrari's thoughts. He hadn't gotten both eyes open before he noticed JuJu's arm extended over his left knee. He jumped with fear.

"What did I do?" He knew what it meant when JuJu went inside the glove compartment after pulling into their garage. Although the sex between he and Tori had been premeditated, JuJu didn't know this and so she had no right to be angry with him. At least that's how he saw it.

JuJu ignored his question. She pulled out a black rectangular device and Ferrari went for the door. It was locked, of course, and in that split second Ferrari felt the shock of JuJu's taser disrupt his muscle control. She laughed wickedly as she watched his big body contract at her will.

"You wanna make a bitch tremble?" she asked. "Well, so do I!"

JuJu sent enough electricity through Ferrari to turn his pretend sleep real. His eyes closed and his head drooped. This was her indication to take her finger off the trigger. She reached over her husband's jittery leg, put the weapon back in the glove compartment, and retrieved a couple napkins. She pulled down the mirror from above the driver's seat and stared at her reflection as she patted the beads of sweat that had gathered across her forehead.

She closed the mirror, balled the napkin, and threw

it at her unconscious husband. She then pressed her thumb into the remote that was clipped to the mirror, bringing the garage door back down. She got out of the car, leaving the keys in the ignition and the engine running, and headed inside.

"That's why I told them we were going to Tahiti," she mumbled, "if you must know." She removed her coat. "I'm gonna need a couple uninterrupted days to get you back in line."

## Lyssa & Jacob

"Uhnnnn, uhnnnn, szzzz," I moaned through my clenched teeth.

I enjoyed all kinds of sexual positions but being scissored was one I'd come to love. And my live-in, Morgan, had it down to a science. She made sure our clitorises were perfectly aligned and then she'd aggressively twirl her hips like she was in a hula-hoop competition. It always made me cum. Tonight was no different.

"Szzzzz, oh God!" I shrieked.

Morgan was sure to keep her movement steady until I was completely done. Stopping midway might be cause for a dock in her pay. She had learned that lesson the first week on the job.

"You done?" Jacob whispered in my ear from his position behind me. His hands were planted on my boobs, fingers paying special attention to my nipples.

I nodded, accompanying my response was a wet kiss. My husband reciprocated. Morgan watched our tongues dance in each other's mouths while she gently stroked Jacob's thigh. It was his turn next.

I sat up, leaning my back against the headboard, and lit a cigarette. The only time I'd ever smoke was after sex. I didn't know why. Jacob wanted me to quit. But I would always tell him, you can't quit a habit you don't have. Seriously, smoking was never a vice of mine. Other than after orgasms, I never even thought about cigarettes.

I puffed and dragged while Morgan gave my husband a blowjob. I watched her jaws expand and contract with every motion. Jacob's hand palmed the crown of her head like it was a basketball. I didn't know if he was guiding her movement or just following it. His face was scrunched up like he couldn't stand it, yet I knew he loved every minute. Just like he used to with me. I couldn't remember the last time I had given my husband head, but I did remember how much he used to enjoy it.

Since we started hiring live-ins, two years earlier when our youngest went away to college, my wifely duties had been cut down significantly. And where sex used to be a chore for me, live-ins made it pleasurable—as pleasurable as it had always been for my husband. Now we were on a level playing field. Our sex drives were compatible, thus our love life was incredible.

It was that very change in momentum that had brought the urge to open a swingers club. We wanted other couples to get to that same space of complete sexual fulfillment. And Puss & Boots was just the place that allowed this to happen. The name was our first choice, and although we considered others, we stuck with our gut. We used our retirement money to open it, and it turned out to be one of the best investments we'd ever made. Who knew so many people, from all walks of life, would be into swapping partners?

Two years and one hundred fifty memberships later, we were able to live good off our club, and when I say good, I mean we could afford extras like a housekeeper, a daily dining-out habit, and of course our live-ins.

Live-ins got five hundred a week plus they stayed with us rent-free. All their utilities including cable and Internet were taken care of. Meals, cell phone, and car expenses were on us. A live-in paid only for her personal hygiene items and outings or trips she wanted to go on without us. That way, she could save up for a place of her own, for tuition, or for whatever else she wanted to do. In exchange, Jake and I got sex on demand. It was a win-win.

We usually hired a different live-in every two or three months. That was about how long they generally needed to accumulate enough money for whatever it was they were trying to achieve. For us, it helped in preventing boredom.

We met our first live-in when we were in New Orleans. We had gone down there one year for the Essence Music Festival and one night we got entirely too drunk. We dipped into one of the many clubs that line Bourbon Street to retreat from the ninety-degree heat.

We didn't even realize until we were shoving dollar bills down a girl's thong that we were in a *strip* club. It was all a drunken blur. At some point we got a lap dance from a girl from Atlanta, our hometown. Indeed, she was the first girl to ever make me second-guess my sexuality. We spent the rest of our night getting lap dances from her. Then we invited her to our hotel room. We had the best sex. We paid her well and I made a simple comment that would change our lives for good.

"I wish I could take you home with me," I said, joking but serious.

"You can," was her response. "Are you two into having a live-in?"

Neither Jake nor I knew what that was. A nanny was the first thing that came to my mind.

"Both our kids are grown and out of the house," I told her.

"That's perfect—we won't have to hide from anybody."

Then I understood that what she was referring to had nothing to do with babysitting. Jacob and I took her number. We discussed it at breakfast, lunch, and dinner the next day. We weighed pros and cons. By the time we landed back in Atlanta three days later, we were calling the girl to set it up.

Her name was Jasmine. She had moved to New Orleans to live with a boyfriend after high school. He became abusive and she left him. Stripping was a way for her to support herself. But it wasn't panning out the way she'd hoped. She had heard of girls getting more money and stability by becoming live-ins to wealthy couples. She wanted that opportunity for herself. And Atlanta was familiar territory for her, so we fit the bill.

She moved in with us a month after she had danced her way into our lives. She showed us so much about sex and how to achieve true ecstasy. She was a gift. She left us at the end of three months, but not before she showed us how to look for our next live-in.

There were two websites she introduced us to, TheRedLightCenter.com and SwingLifestyle.com. The first one caught Jake and I totally off guard. It's a virtual world of partying, drinking, vacationing, socializing, and of course having sex with random people. You create an avatar that is very lifelike. Then you virtually interact with people as you would in the real world. You find someone compatible for you and you end up having virtual sex with him or her and, if interested, you can arrange to meet in person and have actual live sex. A lot of people in our lifestyle go on that site to find fuck buddies.

It was intriguing, but Jake and I found SwingLifestyle.com to be more our speed. First of all, it was filled with single females. Second of all, it was simple. You sign up to be a member, set up a profile, and seek out single females who fit the bill. You can find parties, groups, clubs, and even read stories by other swingers. There had been many occasions where Jake and I had gotten extremely horny simply visiting the site.

It was the best resource Jasmine could've led us to. And every time we went on SwingLifestyle to search out our next prospect, I thought about her, wondering if her profile would pop up.

Anyway, Jacob and I adapted to our new lifestyle quite well. While we were comfortable with it and open in our own way, our children didn't know about it. Neither did the rest of our family or close friends. Only our live-ins and our Puss & Boots members. We liked it that way. A double life wasn't as hard to lead as we initially feared. And it actually made the whole thing more exciting. We were content.

\* \* \*

Jake's body jolted. He was cumming. I put out my cigarette and joined Morgan at the base of my husband's penis. She licked one side, I did the other, our tongues collecting his semen. We swallowed and then kissed each other, passionately, sloppily. We caressed and then nibbled on each other's breasts. This got us all aroused again. Jake positioned me on all fours and, parting my lips, entered me from behind. Morgan placed her lower half beneath my face and began sliding her fingers up and down her slit. Watching her kept me good and lubricated for my husband's pleasure. We were both headed toward a second orgasm and there was no better way to spend my Saturday night.

# CHAPTER 2

# THANKSGIVING DISGUISED AS A FEAST

## Tori & Kevin

THE DRIVE TO MY MOM'S HOUSE reminded me of just how much I loved the fall. The collage of orange and red leaves glowing in the sunlight always made me think of my childhood. I imagined myself playing in the orchards, running through the corn maze trying to lose my dad, eating candy corn, and picking out the biggest pumpkin I could find. It made me smile. I missed my dad. It had been a year since his death. In fact, two life-changing developments had occurred within that last year: my wedding, then two days later the passing of my father. That was the reason I agreed to marry Kevin so quickly after his proposal in the first place. My father was ill and we all knew he didn't have much time. It meant everything to him to walk his only daughter down the aisle. So despite not being ready for marriage, I recited my vows in front of eighty-five of Kevin and my closest family members and friends.

*Beep! Beep! Beep!*

The horn took me away from my memories. It was Kevin's way of announcing our arrival. He did it every time we pulled up to my mom's brick ranch home. Now she was ill too. Her sight was failing her. So Kevin and I were trying to spend as much time with her as possible, especially during holidays.

It was Thanksgiving Day and she had managed to cook us up a traditional turkey feast. Cooking was something my mom excelled at. She could do it with her eyes closed, let alone legally blind.

I jumped out the passenger seat and hurried down the rest of the driveway to my mother's doorstep, where she stood with her arms out waiting to greet us with warm hugs.

"Happy Thanksgiving, Mama." I kissed her on her cheek as we embraced.

"Happy Thanksgiving, baby." She kissed me back.

"Hey, Mom." Kevin hugged and kissed her next. "You're looking good." She loved his compliments, said he was just like my dad in that way. It was probably why she always thought Kevin was so perfect for me.

"Are you two hungry?" she asked, leading us into the home I grew up in.

"Starving," Kevin said. He had taken a strong liking to my mom as well. She filled the void of him not having his own mother.

In the beginning of our relationship Kevin hardly ever talked about his mom, and whenever I asked about her, he'd cut the conversation short. It wasn't until later that I found out she had died of a drug overdose when he was a teenager. I felt sorry for him, knowing that it had a huge impact on him. So when he and my mom connected, it was electric. He was the son she never had and she was the mom he'd always wished he had. I couldn't have asked for a better situation.

"Tori, honey, set the table. Kevin, go wash your hands," my mom instructed.

We did what we were told, parting ways briefly. It was right then that my phone alerted me to a text message. I looked down at the screen and saw that it was from him. I hadn't heard from him since our first physical encounter a week ago. A bit of excitement ran through my veins, but also nervousness. I had a short window of time before Kevin would emerge from the bathroom. I opened the message.

## JuJu & Ferrari

His skin tone flushed and veins popping out of his head, Ferrari thumbed away at the keyboard on his cell phone.

*I can't take it anymore. It's getting worse and worse. What are we waiting for? We finally met each other in person. We finally made love. You still love me after that? Then what are we waiting for?*

He stood up off the king-sized platform bed. He tossed his phone on the stark white duvet cover and rubbed his hands over his head from front to back, pacing the master suite. He anxiously waited for the beep that would let him know she had responded to his text.

He made his way over to the floor-to-ceiling window that separated him from Atlanta. It was ironic that he felt trapped in such a big, open city. But that was how JuJu made him feel. Between the verbal and physical abuse and the threats to have him deported to his native country of Brazil, Ferrari often felt helpless. Sometimes he looked at that window and imagined himself jumping out.

He walked back over to the bed and picked up his phone. No response. He worried that too much time had passed since the last time they communicated. Was that all she had wanted from him? Or had she moved on? He logged onto Facebook. Maybe she had messaged him. That was more private than texting back and forth. He needed to hear from her.

*Don't think it was my choosing to not get in touch with you before now. She did it again. Almost killed me this time. Then held me up at the lake house for four days with no food and no cell service. She just brought me back to the condo. And only so she could entertain guests at the lake house for Thanksgiving dinner. She told everybody I flew home for the holidays. But the truth is, she locked me in here. If I leave I will have no way of getting back in. I hope you understand. It is she who is the problem. Not you. Not me. If you tell me you still love me, I will take away the problem once and for all. I just need to hear from you. Please.*
*Ferrari*

He pressed *Send* on his phone and grew even more anxious. He paced some more, starting to shake from the desperation, fatigue, and anger. He took a seat. He bit away at his thumbnail. He looked at his phone: no alerts, no replies. His heart was beginning to hurt. Not physically but spiritually. He was there alone on Thanksgiving in misery while JuJu was up at the lake house probably at the head of the table for twelve laughing, telling stories of her modeling days, and having a good time.

He could picture the scene. He imagined it was how it used to be when she was courting him. Her charismatic smile and laugh cheered the entire room back then. She was a big personality and Ferrari, not so much. He was an introvert, so being with JuJu helped keep him in the shadows, where he was most comfortable. Little did he know then that this was exactly what JuJu preyed on.

JuJu spotted Ferrari at a friend's dinner party years back in the Hollywood Hills. He was hired as eye candy. At that time, he was a struggling model/actor and JuJu was already an accomplished supermodel. The fact that she showed any interest in the nineteen-year-old was enough to make him do whatever she asked. He was smitten in the way a young boy might be over a teacher he found attractive.

JuJu walked over to him and lifted a glass of champagne off the tray he was holding. Then she took the entire tray and set it on a nearby table. Grabbing a second glass from the tray, she handed one to Ferrari and asked—well, told him—"Take a walk with me."

She led Ferrari to a quiet corner near the back of the pool where the rest of Hollywood was in view. She introduced herself and asked Ferrari what his dreams were. He chuckled. She thought he was being bashful, but really, he didn't have any dreams as of yet. He was just trying to survive, trying to make money the best way he knew how—with his striking looks and rock-hard body. She caught on.

"You don't know, do you?" She lifted his chin to peer into his eyes. "You don't know what you want to do with the rest of your life? Well, that's understandable. You're a baby. What are you, like twenty, twenty-one?"

Ferrari nodded, "Something like that."

"Well, I'll tell you what, why don't you spend some time with me? I can help you figure out your dreams through living them," she proposed. "Anything you can wish for, you name it. A sports car, a home like this." She extended her arm toward the back of the modern mansion. "Whatever you like. Just take care of me and I will take care of you."

It seemed like an easy decision, but Ferrari didn't make it. Instead, he chuckled again. He didn't think the woman was serious. He thought she might have had too much to drink.

JuJu took that as a yes, sure. And she locked her arm in his. "You're mine now, okay?"

He chuckled for a third time.

Eleven years later and Ferrari lived the true meaning of that phrase daily. He was JuJu's the way a slave was his master's.

Ferrari's phone chirped. He had a Facebook message.

*I do still love you. Just need more time to figure things*

*out. Happy you're okay. But with my family now so I
gotta go.*
*Tori*

Ferrari cradled his phone with both hands and ex-
haled. At least there was a sliver of joy to be felt that day.
It was no family dinner, but it was hope.

## Danielle & Stewart

"Look how many people are logged in," I told my husband as I twirled my lo mein on my fork. "You would
think these jerk-offs would be spending time with their
families right now."

"Never complain about business, honey," Stewart
said, not even bothering to glance over at the number of
people now visiting our candid porn site. "Besides, why
do you think the movie theaters are still open on days
like Thanksgiving and Christmas? It's entertainment,
and people are always looking for entertainment, especially during the holidays when the stress of work and
everyday commitments are lifted off them."

I took a forkful of noodles to my mouth. "You've
got a point," I said, chewing. "That's why I married
you. You're so smart and so sexy . . ." I put the Chinese

food down on the desk beside the mouse my husband was running across the mouse pad. Over his shoulder, I watched as he browsed our site. "All this sex is turning me on." I gently massaged his broad shoulders.

Stewart smiled. He loved that I loved him so much. His last wife didn't. In fact, she didn't love men period. She was an undercover lesbian who had married Stew because she thought it was the thing to do. Then at a swingers party once, she took off with a woman and never looked back. She left Stew high and dry. A week later, Stew's circle of swinging friends convinced him to go to a single's night at a club they all were members of. It was where we met. We hit if off almost instantly. And the love and affection I showered him with overwhelmed him—to the point where it was as if he was under my spell. In little time I could get Stewart to do anything I asked, including marrying me and starting our business. He was putty in my hands. But that was okay with him because he knew I would take good care of him. I wasn't out to hurt him. I wasn't using him. I was just a fun, fiery girl who liked to party and fuck.

"Let me just finish this up and I can take that edge off you."

"Okay, hurry," I said, backing away from him.

I headed over to the bar that took up the wall opposite the L-shaped desk my husband was seated at. It was well stocked with top-shelf liquor, various pills, and a small pile of my favorite doctrine, cocaine. I bent down in front of it, then used my thumb to close my right nostril, and with my left, I sniffed as much of the white powder as I could. I wanted to be in a trance. It made sex that much better.

"You know what's more puzzling than the amount of people logged on right now?" Stewart's voice sounded over the light music that played in my mind.

I danced like a ballerina in the middle of our two-story office/library. "What's that? What could be more puzzling?" I smiled.

"That Texas couple got more views than all our other videos. It's like the damn thing went viral. Almost four hundred thousand views in a week."

"Maybe people got a thing for cowboys," I giggled. "Now why don't you get off that thing and let's make a video of our own?"

I returned to the bar, bent down, and snorted some more. By the time I stood back upright, my husband was already inserting himself into me.

I laughed and jerked with pleasure. My nude body was reflected in the mirrored bar and I watched myself get fucked like it was a video on our site. I performed too: I rubbed my breasts and brought them up to my mouth. I sucked my own nipples, eyeing Stew in the mirror while I did it. He cracked a smile. Then he took one hand away from my hip and put it on top of my head, pushing it downward. I guess he didn't want me looking at him. Maybe it was intimidating. I obliged and kept my head lowered—made it easier to get to the coke. And if you've ever snorted while being fucked doggy style, you know I was in my glory.

"Happy Thanksgiving, sexy motherfucker!" I muffled up to my husband, biting my bottom lip. "Happy Thanksgiving . . ."

# Lyssa & Jacob

Robin Thicke's "Blurred Lines" blared through the Bose in-wall speakers. A soul train line was in full swing. One of my sisters, the one who decided to host Thanksgiving dinner that year, was going down the middle clapping and throwing her hips from side to side. The members of my family bordering the dance floor cheered her on.

I was sitting in a recliner by the fireplace laughing and bopping my head, singing along: *"But you're a good girllll, the way you grab me, must wanna get nasty, go 'head get at me . . ."*

Jake was at the card table playing blackjack with my sisters' husbands and a couple nephews. The music, cheering, dancing, and laughter went largely unnoticed by them. They all had serious looks on their faces, concentrated on the cards and money on the table.

At the dining table the latecomers were eating from whatever was left. My son, Jacob Jr., and his wife and child were among them. I glanced over from time to time in admiration at the family my son had built. Watching him feed my grandbaby was surreal. It felt like just yesterday that it was me feeding him.

Meanwhile, my daughter Alexandria was sitting beside Morgan on the couch making small talk. At first I was worried, but Morgan was pretty careful with her words so I felt comfortable that nothing would slip out. Besides, when Jake and I agreed to let Morgan join us for Thanksgiving, we all went over our story numerous times until it was embedded in our brains. We told everybody that Morgan was our new receptionist down at the assisted living residence they all thought we owned. She didn't have much family of her own so we invited her to spend the holiday with ours. The latter part of our story was actually true.

It worked; no one questioned it. They welcomed her as they would have welcomed anybody. That's how my family is. Very warm, friendly, and accepting. Well, to a degree. Jake and I were certain they wouldn't be so warm and friendly to Morgan had they knew her real position.

My song ended and the soul train came to its last stop. My relatives trickled off the dance floor and filled the seats throughout my sister's home. My son and his family were finished eating. I figured this was the perfect time to start putting dishes in the washer and wrapping up some of the food so that we could put the dessert out. I called on my daughter to help me. This would also get me caught up on her third semester at Hampton University.

"I'm stuffed. How about you?" I asked her as we entered the kitchen.

"I could go for dessert," she said.

"Yeah, I think everyone could, which is why I wanted to put some of this food away to make room for your aunt's famous banana pudding."

"Mom . . ."

"Yes?"

"How long has that girl Morgan been working for you and Daddy?"

I swallowed. "A little while now, why?"

"I don't know. She seems a little . . ."

"A little what?" I avoided eye contact with my daughter.

"I think she may like Daddy."

I couldn't help but laugh. I looked up at her. "That's funny. What gave you that impression?"

"The way she brought him his beer while he was playing cards. And when we were in grace, I saw her peep up at Daddy. She just seems a little flirty toward him."

"Nooo," I shook my head. "She's just trying very hard to appease him. He *is* her boss. She just wants to impress him, is all."

"You're her boss too and I don't see her trying to appease you."

"Yeah, but your dad and I have two different roles down at the home. He's the one who runs it, I just do the financing. So in reality, he's her boss, not me." Truth be told, I did start wondering why Morgan was acting one way toward Jake and another toward me. We had equal stock in her. Neither Jake nor I wanted her more than the other and it was supposed to be that way on her end too.

I brushed it off for the time being and got back to putting food and dishes away with my daughter. But I had made a mental note to keep an eye on Miss Morgan.

# CHAPTER 3

# NEVER FUCK NOBODY WITHOUT TELLIN' ME

## Tori & Kevin

IT HAD BEEN A LITTLE OVER A MONTH since Kevin and I had our first swinging experience. And it had taken that long for us to get completely over the ordeal. Although we'd concluded that we were both all right with what we had done, neither of us was really able to shake the awkward feelings. Kevin still carried insecurities about not being able to make me orgasm. And me, well, I felt guilty.

I tried convincing myself that because it was something we both did together, it was okay. But I knew better. I knew what I was doing. I acted like it was a surprise for Kevin's birthday. But the truth was, Ferrari and I had planned it that way.

You see, I met Ferrari online right after Kevin and I got married. It started out innocently enough. Just a couple comments on each other's statuses and photos—nothing more, nothing less. Then one night he had confided in me via an inbox message about being in an abusive relationship. How his wife controlled him, manipulated him, and degraded him. I felt sorry for him and tried to console him. He began to grow feelings for me. Then I for him. In time, we were creating fake Facebook pages just so we could message each other every day without being caught by our spouses.

Seven months into it, I had become one of those people I used to doubt: the ones who claim to have fallen in love with a person they've never seen or met.

One day Ferrari proposed we finally meet up. He chose a day, time, and meeting place. I was a no-show. I had gotten cold feet. I was worried about hurting Kevin. Two months and deep sexual feelings later, I agreed to Ferrari's master plan. He had told me that he and his wife went to a swingers club on occasion. It was his wife's way of tormenting him, making him watch her have sex with other guys. She told him he didn't do it for her. She needed to find a man who did. In exchange, she would let him have sex with other women. And she would taunt him for not being able to make any of the women cum. It was his flaw, she told him. And she would ask, "How could such a good looking man be so bad at making love?"

Ferrari wanted to get even with her. As for me, I wanted to have guilt-free sex with Ferrari. And since Kevin and I had jokingly talked about trying a threesome or engaging in group sex, I figured taking him to a swingers club for his birthday was the perfect gift—for both of us.

Turns out it made things even more complicated. But then, just when I felt like our complicated feelings were fading and we were getting back to normalcy, Ferrari inboxed me about an annual Christmas party being hosted by a Puss & Boots member. He wanted me to come. And I wanted to see him again. But I knew it was wrong so I tried to ignore it. I deleted the message, figuring if it were out of sight it would be out of mind. But that didn't work because a few days later I went into the trash and retrieved it. I told myself that it would be just one more time. That as long as I stuck to Kevin and my principles and only did it together, there would be no harm.

I waited about a week after seeing the message and contemplating whether or not we should attend before I brought it up with Kevin. We were at P.F. Chang's having dinner.

"So I got an e-mail about a Christmas party at a Puss & Boots member's mansion," I came right out after sipping my wonton soup.

Kevin looked up from his plate of dynamite shrimp. "Oh yeah?" he asked plainly. "Which member?" He took a bite out of one of the crispy appetizers.

"A couple named Mr. and Mrs. Oxford. Apparently they're a big deal."

"When is it?"

"The Saturday after Christmas."

"You wanna go?"

"It sounds like it's goin' be bananas. Live shows and everything."

He nodded his head. "We can check it out," he said, surprising me by not needing any convincing. "But if we see that couple we go the other way, deal?"

"Definitely," I agreed easily with my mouth, but there was anxiety in my gut.

The night of the party, Kevin and I hit Cheetah's. It was not as entertaining as the other strip clubs in Atlanta, but it served its purpose. We got drunk and horny.

We took a cab to the address in the Christmas party e-mail. We were too inebriated to drive ourselves—and getting home, forget about it.

When we arrived at the Oxford home it was like we had pulled up in front of the Disney castle. The place was huge and lit up to holiday perfection.

We were a couple hours late—on purpose. And from the amount of cars parked on the street and in the driveway, it appeared that the place was packed. Kevin paid and tipped the cab driver and we got out. We walked up the lighted pathway to the front door. As soon as I thumbed the bell, the eight-foot doors opened up.

A security guard patted us each down and a butler type replaced our coats with plush robes. A third and fourth person checked our cell phones in and gave us a confidentiality agreement to sign. All this just to get past the grand foyer, and when we did, we entered something even the imagination would have trouble drawing up.

It was like Winter Wonderland meets Cirque du Soleil with a touch of Medieval Times. Two naked female acrobats did flips and tricks on a trampoline in the center of the two-story great room. Meanwhile, off in a corner, two buff guys were acting out a duel. Fake snow and bubbles shot out of machines strategically placed throughout the house. Music pumped through the in-wall speakers. The Weeknd's album *Trilogy*, to be specific.

In the formal dining room there was a woman laid out on the table. Sushi decorated her nude body in such a way that it looked sophisticated, artistic. Between her thighs stood a fountain of spiked sweet tea. We didn't need any more to drink, but Kevin and I helped ourselves to a cup anyway.

In the kitchen, three chefs were preparing endless trays of exotic finger foods. A couple steps down in a theater area, a live sex show was taking place. An Asian dominatrix was whipping her male counterpart with a leather strap while shoving an oversized dildo into his anal cavity.

Kevin and I peeked in and backed out of the theater. That wasn't our thing. Around the corner, in the library, a sex therapist was selling and demonstrating sex toys and gadgets.

A woman participant was lying on her back on the floor. There were two additional women holding her thighs open. The sex therapist was sitting Indian style between the woman's legs, passing a vibrating device over her vagina. The woman's eyes were rolled in the back of her head. Her mouth was parted, allowing harmonious sounds to pour out. There were times she tried to get up to resist the pleasure, but another pair of women who were caressing and licking her breasts would gently hold her down. Meanwhile the audience of mostly women were watching intensely, some moaning and fingering themselves or the person next to them. It was definitely a turn-on.

Just when we thought we had seen it all, we noticed a huge white tent beyond the sliding-glass doors. We followed the rose petal–covered walkway down to the entrance of the tent. Thankfully we were given the robes. The December air was unfriendly to us warm-blooded beings.

The inside of the tent resembled a Michelangelo

fresco. Dozens upon dozens of bare bodies were piled upon each other in the biggest orgy I'd ever seen. Kevin looked at me, his eyes wide, mouth open. He couldn't believe it. Neither could I, but I was at least able to play it off.

Instantly, the walls of my vagina started to pulsate. I felt an intense need to be touched. My eyes became lasers, zeroing in on some of the lewd acts that were happening around us. I imagined myself in some of the women's positions. I licked my lips as I watched a woman deep throat a man. Her mouth was opened real wide as she made his entire penis disappear and reappear with each suck. The man's lips were pursed as he took short, quick breaths. Veins were popping out of pretty much every body part. His knees were slightly bent and his hands were securely planted on the woman's head.

Meanwhile, another woman wearing a strap-on was penetrating the deep throater. That woman's big plump breasts were bouncing up and down to the rhythm of her quick, short strokes which matched the guy's panting. I couldn't help but rub my own titties.

Kevin joined me. He came behind me, slipping his hands under my robe and up to my nipples. I could feel his erection poking me in my lower back. I was so wet by then and I wanted him inside of me. I bent over, right there in that tight space by the tent's entrance, as he guided his dick into my hole.

"Ahhhh." The sexual tension I had built up since the strip club was easing.

We made our way down to our knees, doing it doggy style. This way, we were closer to the action. I could reach out just a little and my hand would be resting upon a woman's breast or a man's dick. It was that packed in there.

A loud sigh soared over the melodious groans that provided the soundtrack for the moment. It came from a woman whose pussy was being chomped by an older woman. *I want that feeling*, I thought as I stared at the oral showdown.

Kevin was quick, about four minutes or so. I expected it though. So the next round would last, hopefully long enough for me to tremble. That's when I thought about Ferrari, and it hit me that without our cell phones we wouldn't be able to text each other our whereabouts. Maybe Kevin would get his wish after all.

When he exited me, we embraced and kissed. We were ready for more, but first we needed to wipe ourselves clean. We left the tent and headed back inside the house to the nearest bathroom.

"You can go first," Kevin said. Gesturing at the bar, he added, "I'll be right over there."

The bathroom was around a tight corner. Just as I escaped Kevin's view, I almost had a head-on collision with . . . *him*. We had found each other. Shit, we had found each other.

"Finally," he said, his eyes adjusting to the fact that it was me he had almost plowed into. "I've been looking everywhere for—"

Before he could say another word I placed my finger over his mouth. I didn't want Kevin or anybody else to hear chatter coming from the hallway.

We entered the bathroom letting our eyes do the talking. That awkward, powerless feeling a girl gets in front of the guy who she lost her virginity to overcame me. I had thought I'd outgrown those types of juvenile emotions, but that was the thing: Ferrari made me feel young all over again.

Inside the bathroom there was a toilet, a shower stall, and a sink. Everything was dainty, modern, slender. The color scheme was metallic silver and crystals. I watched silently as Ferrari locked the door, then I backed against the shower door, my legs parted slightly. The Weeknd's rendition of "Dirty Diana" played in the background. I was in a dangerous position. Powerless.

Ferrari led with a kiss. Just a peck on my lips at first. He waited for me to resist. I respected that. But when I didn't, he went for it, pushing his tongue into my mouth. I welcomed it, and in a matter of seconds we were clasped to one another, one of his hands on the back of my head, the other squeezing my butt cheek.

We had a short window of time and a lot of unfinished business. There was no sense in beating around the bush. This was our moment to get what we had been longing for. And we took it.

Ferrari picked me up and I wrapped my legs around his waist. My back was supported against the shower stall door. He wasted no time entering me. Looking me in my eyes as he thrust his lower half upward, he was mesmerizing.

I felt the tip of his penis hitting a dead end inside me. It could go no further, but with each of Ferrari's hard thrusts, it tried. Meanwhile, I clawed away at his back, I gripped his butt, and I swung my arms around his neck—all reactions to the painful yet sensual gratification he was lending me.

I held in my yelps as best I could. He mumbled three words over and over, both of us aware enough of our surroundings that we knew to control our volume. I felt his knees buckle a little beneath my body weight and I knew it was that time.

"Don't stop," I whispered. "I'm almost there." I pressed down on his butt, making sure he stayed inside me. He tried to resist; I felt him backing away. I used all the strength I had to keep him thrusting. I was so close to reaching my peak. Then, unable to take it anymore, he exploded inside me. And a second later I trembled. I wasn't wearing a watch but I could tell that it had happened more quickly than before. Either he was getting better or our chemistry stronger.

Either way, we made use of the hundred-square-foot marble-tiled space the only way two shameful adulterers could.

*Knock knock.*

And it hit me, it hit us: we were in the wrong place at the wrong time. We snapped out of our golden trance and disengaged as quietly as we could. We peered at each other with the same question in mind, I figured: *What do we do?*

*Knock knock.*

"Who is it?" Ferrari asked.

I shook my head. I just knew it was Kevin checking on me. And what would he think, hearing a male voice come from the bathroom he'd just watched his wife go into? I was in deep shit. The kind that couldn't be flushed.

"It's Danielle," a woman's voice sounded through the door. "Take your time."

I was relieved, but still on alert. It was time to go. But before I turned the lock on the door I had to know something.

"How did we let it get this far?" I whispered to him.

"We didn't," he answered. "It's our destiny. Just like us bumping into each other tonight. It's what God has planned for us. The only question we should be asking ourselves is how come we're fighting it?"

"Goodnight, Ferrari," I whispered, then walked out the door.

I had tunnel vision when I got out of the bathroom and at the end of it was Kevin. I needed to get to him before he came looking for me. I didn't even notice the woman who had knocked on the door standing right outside. She didn't let me slip past, though.

"Wow, you have a deep voice to be so beautiful."

I snickered.

"I'm Danielle, by the way, the hostess." She extended her delicate hand. "Welcome to my home."

"Nice to meet you," I replied, placing my sweaty palm in hers. "Tori." I immediately regretted telling her my name.

Then Ferrari emerged from the bathroom with a baffled look on his face. He had to be wondering why I was still out there. I wondered that myself. I should have kept it moving.

Danielle's lips spread wide. "Oh, *that's* where that powerful voice came from."

Ferrari shook his head.

I took the opportunity to get out of that hallway and

take Kevin somewhere as far away from Danielle, Ferrari, and that section of the house as possible.

## Danielle & Stewart

"Toast to a very Merry Christmas!" I clinked my champagne glass against everyone's glasses.

"Cheers!" some said.

"Merry Christmas!" said others.

I drank the rest of my rosé gleefully. "Tonight was a good night," I smiled. "I finally got my pussy cat eaten by the boss of all bosses." I chuckled, glancing over at Lyssa.

She gave me the finger, which was so appropriate.

"Next time," I told her. "Baby steps."

Everybody let out a drunken laugh. The party was over, but a few of our close friends stayed behind to have one last drink with us. We were gathered in the rec room on the terrace level of my home. Partial nudity, disheveled hair, and smeared lipstick was all evidence of the fun we'd had that night.

"Where's your third wheel?" I asked Lyssa.

JuJu, one of the more experienced of our group, mumbled, "I knew somebody was missing."

"Shockingly, she went to visit some distant relatives

for Christmas," Lyssa replied, shooting a strange look at her husband. "She won't be back until after the New Year."

Jacob seemed a bit uncomfortable, but I was under the influence so I might have been imagining things. I decided to make a joke of it.

"Well, I'm happy for her," I slurred. "I'm sure she could use a break. You work the hell outta that little girl. Aren't there some child labor laws you two should be adhering to?"

The group laughed, including Lyssa and Jacob.

"Aye, JuJu, I see you and Ferrari got yourselves ahold of the new couple . . ."

JuJu gave a confused expression, then Ferrari turned to her and mumbled, "Yeah, remember last month, at the club." He hurriedly sought refuge in his champagne glass.

JuJu nodded, "Yeah, but how did you know about that, Danielle? We didn't see you that night until we were getting dressed."

"I saw Ferrari and what's her name, Tori, come out of the bathroom together tonight." I smiled and winked at Ferrari.

"You saw *what?*" JuJu asked.

*Shit,* I thought. I didn't say anything. Instead, I took my glass to my lips. And even though it was empty, I threw my head back.

Ferrari stepped in. "She was coming in as I was walking out. We spoke to each other and that was that."

JuJu didn't believe him—it was written all over her Botoxed face. Don't be mistaken, JuJu was beautiful. She was a retired supermodel for Christ's sake. But like most of us, she worried about aging, and so from time to time she'd get Botox injections to keep everything pulled and tight.

"Okay, so which one was it, you two came out of the bathroom together or you came out and she went in?"

"I came out and she went in."

JuJu looked at me. "But you said you saw them both come out together."

I laughed. I was too unstable to be serious. But I did know how to diffuse the situation. "I don't know what I saw. I've been drunk all night."

"Anyway," Lyssa jumped in, "why would there ever be a trust issue with a couple who swings? You're getting everything you could possibly want without having to sneak around, so . . . ."

Jacob glanced at his wife with that same uneasiness as before. But I dared not speak on it. Hell, I hadn't yet put out the first fire I started. I just clinked my empty glass with my husband's. Meanwhile JuJu and Ferrari sat tight-lipped. It was awkward as hell for the remainder of the night. A prelude to an ending none of us saw coming.

## JuJu & Ferrari

Ferrari's plan was to go straight to bed to avoid any confrontation with JuJu. While she was in the shower he stripped down to his underwear. He pulled back the covers that were tightly tucked under the mattress and climbed into the bed. He said a silent prayer and closed his eyes.

He heard the shower stop running and said another prayer. He hoped that JuJu was too tired to bring up the cat Danielle had let out of the bag.

JuJu's footsteps neared their bed and then stopped. What was she doing? He carefully opened one eyelid halfway. He could see JuJu's silhouette above him, and suddenly a bucket of scalding-hot water came pouring down over him. A stinging pain pierced his entire body as he leapt to his feet.

"AHHHHHH! AHHHH!" Ferrari tried running from the assault, but between the slippery marble floor and his shaking body, he slammed down to the ground.

JuJu stood over him, beating him with the bucket. "Who do you think you are that you have the audacity to go off and fuck that girl in MY friend's home while I'M right in the next room?" She lost grip of the bucket and it went flying across the bedroom.

Ferrari slid toward the bed and leaned back against the platform, but JuJu didn't let up. She continued beating him with her fists. With each blow, Ferrari forced a flashback of Tori and him making love. It was his only means of escaping the abuse—he had to put his mind in a whole different space.

As JuJu struck him, he imagined Tori. The look on her face as he penetrated her. The feeling he had not just in his manhood but also in his heart, in his soul, as he pleased her. Soon the pain subsided. JuJu's rants began to lose steam. He closed his eyes and stayed in his own mind.

But then JuJu seemed to gain a second wind, striking Ferrari with more intensity and hatred than she ever had before. She was actually causing his skin to break. Blood began to drip from his face. That was the final straw.

Ferrari watched for JuJu's next swing and, with his adrenaline pumping, gripped her arm and flipped her over. She fell on her back on the cold, wet marble floor.

She screamed. Ferrari stood up. He looked at her squirming on the floor. Through tears, blood, and stray water droplets he scanned the room for his phone. He grabbed it off the nightstand and dialed 911. He'd had enough.

He locked himself in the bathroom while he waited

for the cops to come just in case JuJu got her bearings and came after him again. It was a good thing he did too, because as soon as JuJu was able to get back up she went crazy. She grabbed a letter opener from her night-stand drawer and pounded on the bathroom door.

"I'M GONNA KILL YOU! YOU THINK YOU CAN GET AWAY WITH THIS?! HAVE YOU LOST YOUR MIND?! YOU THINK YOU CAN DO THIS TO ME?!"

Ferrari just sat on the toilet seat and waited for the pounding to stop. When it eventually did, that was his cue that the police had arrived. As he crept out of the bathroom he could hear voices. He entered the living room to find JuJu at the door talking to two officers.

When Ferrari approached the door to offer his side of the story, one of the officers stopped him in his tracks. One hand up and the other on the top of his holstered gun, he commanded, "Stop right there."

"But I'm the one who called. She poured hot water on me, beat me, she's tasered me before, she's . . ." Ferrari went down the list.

"What have you done to make her defend herself in those ways?" the other officer asked.

JuJu looked back at him, a smirk on her face. Then she butted in. "Listen, I think this is all one big misunder-standing. We had a little fight tonight that got somewhat out of control. And for the sake of him not being arrested and possibly even deported," she placed emphasis on *deported*, knowing that was a sensitive subject for Ferrari, "I don't want to press any charges and I know he doesn't want to press any charges. I think we both just need to get some rest."

"All right then," the first officer said, taking his hand off his gun.

"That sounds like the best thing, especially if you, sir," he peered at Ferrari, "want to avoid being sent back across the border."

Ferrari was dumbfounded. Then he noticed the folded bills JuJu placed in their hands as they shook on their agreement to leave without making any arrests.

The door to the condo closed and by the time JuJu had turned around to get her hands on Ferrari once more, he was gone. Back in the bathroom behind the locked door. He sat on the toilet seat and typed into his phone: *I'm ready*. Then he pressed *Send*.

## Lyssa & Jacob

"Make sure you dust everything good," I instructed my housekeeper. "Her allergies are a bitch." It was the morning of Morgan's flight back and I was making sure everything was perfect for her. "Jake!" I yelled up to my husband who had just got out of the shower. "Don't mess that bathroom up!" My husband was a true slob. Wherever he removed his clothing was where it would stay. But I wasn't havin' that this morning. Not only was our housekeeper almost done cleaning up, but Morgan was due to land any minute.

"She's not the pope," Jake teased. "And it's goin' to get dirty all over again right after she gets here."

"Boy!" I yelled to hush him.

Just like our family, our cleaning lady didn't know the nature of our real relationship with Morgan. Unlike our family, though, our cleaning lady thought she was our goddaughter who was coming to stay with us to attend school. Morgan had multiple identities to the different people in our lives and I wanted it to stay that way.

"I'm going to the store!" I yelled up, grabbing my pocketbook off the couch. Then I took a couple bills from the zipper pocket and put them on the kitchen counter. "In case I'm not back when you get ready to leave, here's your pay," I told our cleaning lady.

Then I left. I took the elevator to the first floor, walked past the mailboxes, out the door, and I was in the middle of a shopping, dining metropolis. I loved living in the city.

Selling our home in the suburbs was one of the best

decisions Jake and I made after the kids moved out. The money helped toward our business venture and we were able to move to a place where no one knew us. That way, we wouldn't have to worry about neighbors asking questions or popping up at the wrong time.

I walked around the corner to Victoria's Secret and purchased some nice and naughty pieces for that night. Then I stopped in Bath & Body Works to get some candles and oils. Lastly, I went to Publix and picked up their famous Southern-style red velvet cake.

By the time I got back home, our cleaning lady was gone and Morgan was sitting in my living room with Jake.

"Hey!" I said cheerfully, setting my bags down on the counter.

"Hey." Morgan's greeting didn't sound as cheerful.

I looked at Jake and that's when I noticed his face was as sorrowful as Morgan sounded.

"What's wrong?" I asked as I stopped fiddling with the shopping bags. I walked out of the galley kitchen around to the living room, joining my husband and our live-in.

"Morgan has some news," Jake said.

I gave her the floor. I wanted to sit down, but was too anxious. I had no idea what was about to come from her mouth, but I knew from their faces it couldn't be good.

"Lyssa," she started off, "I'm pregnant."

I sat down. Speechless at first, I clutched my necklace. A swarm of questions filled my head. "By who?" came out first. "I mean, Jake always used protection whenever we all . . ." Then a fear revealed itself. I turned to my husband. "You fucked her behind my back, didn't you?"

Jake's jaw dropped. That's when I lost it. I jumped to my feet.

"She's pregnant with your baby, isn't she?!" I got up in his face.

Words struggled to escape his throat. But they didn't have a chance with me.

"Alexandria told me how flirtatious Morgan was with you while we were at my sister's for Thanksgiving!"

Jake's face crumbled in defense.

I kept going: "And is that why she lied and said she was visiting"—I made quotations with my fingers—"'distant relatives' over the Christmas break? But really you put her up in a hotel?"

Jake wondered how I knew about that. At least that's what his face told me.

"Did you forget that I do the finances?!" I yelled at him. "I saw it on your statements, Jake!" I paced the floor, clutching my necklace again. "How long?" I asked, this time my attention going to Morgan.

"Lyssa, noooo," she shook her head. "I've never slept with your husband behind your back. It's always been here or at the club when the three of us were together. The reason why your daughter noticed something between us at Thanksgiving was because that was the day I confided in Jake about being pregnant. I didn't want him to tell you because I knew you would fire me. And the reason he put me up in that hotel was so that I could recover from the abortion that I was going to have . . ." She glanced over at Jake. And so did I.

He bowed his head.

She continued, "But after giving it a lot of thought, I couldn't do it. So here I am, telling you that I'm pregnant, not by your husband, by my boyfriend."

I let go of my chain and sighed with relief. I sat back down and replayed Morgan's explanations in my head. Everything she said made sense. It added up . . . But wait, she wasn't off the hook yet. "Boyfriend?"

Jake looked up at the ceiling and rubbed his goatee.

"I'm sorry, Lyssa, I know that was part of our agreement from the start, to not have sex with anybody else, but—"

"Do you know why my husband and I had you agree to that in the first place?"

She nodded. "You wanted me to yourselves."

I shook my head with disgust. "Not so we could have

you all to ourselves. We needed that commitment from you for our *protection*. When we took you to the doctor and got that clean bill of health from you, it was our understanding that we would both be free and clear of any and all STDs throughout the duration of your job. You goin' out and fuckin' some boyfriend behind our backs put us in a compromising position. Because no longer are we free and clear of anything." I couldn't believe I had to break it down to the girl.

"Well, my boyfriend's clean, I can vouch for him."

"That's not the point, Morgan. That's not the point at all."

"Morgan," Jake finally broke his silence, "just go ahead and get your things. My wife and I need a moment."

Morgan stood up and walked out of the living room. She jogged upstairs.

"I know this is upsetting to you," Jake began. "But let's just be glad it was a boyfriend and not a terrible consequence of our lifestyle, like you suggested." He cleared his throat as a sign that he was looking for me to say something.

"I'm sorry," I muffled. "I just . . ." I searched for the right words. "I got caught up in my fears and then when lies were being told and now this, it just made me snap."

Jake stood up and walked over to me. He grabbed my hands and held them in his. "Apology accepted," he said with a slight grin. Then he pulled me to my feet.

We embraced. And there in his arms, I let my thoughts roam. Jake was right, I had to look at the positive side of this situation. But one thing weighed on me that made this difficult. Certainty. I needed to know for sure the baby was not my husband's. And I needed to know for sure that this boyfriend was in fact clean. A doctor's appointment for both Jake and me would answer the second question in just a matter of weeks. But I'd have to wait months before I could get an accurate answer to the first question. Months of what would feel like a damn prison sentence.

# CHAPTER 4

# DECEPTION IS THE ONLY FELONY

## Tori & Kevin

I T WAS A THUNDERSTORM. Kevin was working late. I had just pulled up to the garage of a lake house I had no business being at. I sat in my car arguing with myself about my decision to go there. What the hell was I doing? I put the car in reverse. I was taking my ass back home.

Then in my rearview I saw another car approaching, blocking me in. The headlights blurred my vision. I pressed my foot on the brake. Squinting, I tried to make out who it was that had pulled up behind me.

Then I saw him. Ferrari. He stepped out of the driver's seat. He was in a T-shirt that got soaked instantly and a pair of jeans. He was carrying a bag in his hands.

I rolled down my window to tell him I'd had a change of heart and that I was going back home. But "You're going to get sick" came out instead.

"I was in and out," he said, cowering from the raindrops. "You coming in, right?"

I wanted to say no. But I knew that would lead to a back-and-forth and I didn't want to keep him in the rain any longer. I figured I'd go in for a second and then say my goodbyes.

I put the car in park, turned it off, and stepped out. I opened my umbrella and shared it with him.

We walked up the driveway together. I could smell that it was food he was carrying. We got to the front door and he opened it with a key. I put the umbrella down and moved inside. He followed.

"It's nasty out there, isn't it," he stated the obvious. "Get comfortable, make yourself at home."

I walked just a few steps in and was in awe. A wall of windows provided a perfect view of Lake Spivey, one of Georgia's many beautiful lakes. A fire was burning in the stone fireplace. And above it hung a large flatscreen that was set to a music channel.

I sat down on a plush sectional. My plans to stay for only a second were diminishing with every comfort.

"You hungry?" Ferrari asked, as he moved the food from the bag onto plates.

"I am now," I said, the aroma delighting my nostrils.

"Good. I got us some soul food."

Soul food was something we learned through our Facebook messaging that we both liked a lot but our spouses didn't care for. Mine because he was somewhat of a health nut. And his because growing up in a white household, she never really developed an appreciation for baked macaroni-and-cheese and candied yams like we had.

"It smells delicious," I told him.

"It's from the best spot in Atlanta," he boasted, almost as if he had cooked it himself.

"You went all the way to Paschal's? In this rain?"

"You said you hadn't had it since you got married and moved away, so I thought I'd treat you to something premarriage," he explained, walking my plate out to me.

As he set down a tray on the ottoman in front of me, I thought back to the conversation we'd had on Facebook about Paschal's. It was one of our first private exchanges, many months ago. I thought it was sweet how he had remembered.

"So what's so important that you called me here? What news do you have for me?" I got right to the point.

Ferrari disregarded my questions. He took his place beside me, grabbed my hand, and blessed the food. We immediately dug in. Our conversation would have to wait until after we ate, I guessed. And that was just fine with me.

Afterward, Ferrari cleaned up our dishes and put his iPhone in its dock. He shuffled through his playlist and found what he was looking for. The sound of thunder clapping outside was a perfect prelude. Then the beat played and I fell under Ferrari's spell.

*You'll never make me stay, so take your weight off of me . . .* The Weeknd's opening line to "D.D." took me back to the bathroom at Danielle and Stewart Oxford's mansion almost three weeks ago. I was powerless.

Ferrari brought me to my feet and pulled me into him. Naturally I rested my head on his chest. We slow-danced around the great room. I muffled the words of the song, closing my eyes to really feel the music. *"That's okay, hey baby, do what you please, I have the stuff that you want, I am that thing that you need . . ."* I sang in a whisper.

Ferrari, seemingly unable to hold back any longer, leaned forward and used his lips to part mine. He stuck his tongue in my mouth. I accepted. We kissed and my body temperature rose. Our hands made their way all over various parts of our bodies. I think he had a fetish for a juicy butt. Thinking back, his wife had a small, tight ass. Mine was voluptuous. My hands rubbed his rock-hard chest. Even through his T-shirt, I could feel the ripples. Before long, my fingers were lifting the shirt off him. And his were pulling my sweats down.

We got completely naked in each other's arms. We grinded, touched, and kissed until we just couldn't take it anymore. Ferrari lifted me up, my thighs wrapped around his waist. He directed his pole to my private entry. I welcomed him. The fire blazed, the thunder roared, the music thumped, and we fucked. It started against the wall for support. Then he stood me up and turned me around. I pressed my hands against the windows to hold myself up while he slid in and out from the back. He came pretty soon but I hadn't yet. So he took me over to the kitchen island and laid me on top of the granite. At first touch, it was cold, but it warmed up quickly. He parted my legs and buried his head there. He blew on my clit and then licked. I clawed his back, I moaned, I clenched my teeth. It felt painfully good.

We ended up on the cowhide rug back in the great room and he was erect again. He lifted my legs up over my head. Years of dance class as a child did wonders for my flexibility. Leaning his body weight on the back of my thighs, he guided himself inside me. Then he pulled out. Then back in. Out. In. Out. In. He was teasing me and it worked because it made me want him like a fiend wants drugs. I got so worked up that by the time he actually left it in and got into a steady rhythm, I was on the verge of climaxing.

"You . . . are . . . are . . . th . . . the . . . best," I panted while my body shook beyond my control.

Winded and satisfied, we lay beside each other and engaged in small talk. First, about how great sex was with each other. Neither one of us had had better. I felt guilty admitting that to Ferrari. I mean, what would my husband think?

Ferrari was less apologetic. He didn't have the same feelings for his wife that I had for Kevin. It was then he told me the reason he begged me to come there.

"I did it," he said.

"Did what?"

"I arranged . . ."

"Arranged what?"

"I'm going to be leaving her soon."

"Are you sure about that?" It wasn't the first time he had made that claim.

"I'm more sure now than I've ever been. You make me feel safe, you know that? I finally feel like I have the courage to be without her."

"Ferrari," I turned my head toward him, "I hope you're not using me as an excuse to leave your wife. I mean, this right here, what we're doing, what we have, it's temporary. The fact of the matter is I'm married. You're married. We can't really think it's best to leave the people we made our vows to just so that we can have great sex."

"Sex is the last thing I'm doing this for. If it were about sex, Tori, I would never leave my wife. She lets me, damn near forces me, to have sex with plenty of women. This is about my happiness. About my pride.

About my security. About my life. My wife is incredibly abusive, as I told you—"

"Then why now?" I cut him off. "From what you've told me, she's been abusive for years, before I came into the picture, so why is it that you're so steadfast on leaving her now? It's me, isn't it?"

"It's timing, to be exact. In the past I was living in fear. I had nowhere to go. I had no one to talk to about what I was going through. I felt alone. But then I met you, and without even knowing, you gave me back pieces of myself that I had lost. You made me remember that I deserved to be happy and feel good about myself. You came at the right time. Because I was on the brink of just ending it. And I saw your status: *One is not wealthy until he has things money cannot buy.* It rang so true. There I was for years accepting abuse because I was so caught up by all the money, the homes, the cars, the clothes, that I told myself, *I could deal with a little bit of pain in exchange for so much pleasure.* When in reality I was slowly deteriorating, selling my soul to the devil because I felt like she was all I had."

I kept quiet, taking in his words like they were a medicine. I felt for him.

"But my eyes are open now. I want to be done. I need to be done. For my sanity, I need this nightmare to be over," he concluded.

I stared up at him. I noticed a tear roll down his face and wiped it away. It did something to me more than his words. I had never seen a grown man cry about being treated so badly by a woman. I was used to it being the other way around. My emotions were getting intense. I had already developed basic feelings for Ferrari over the course of our online relationship, and then the chemistry that sparked between us when we had sex for the first time had heightened them. Now, I was getting to see his vulnerability, his desperate cry for help, and it was making me want to give him all of me. I hugged him—well, squeezed him. I cried with him.

"I love you, Tori," he said tearfully. "And I hope you love me the same because what I am about to do is for us. It's for us to go off and start a new life together. We will have a nice sum of money to go wherever in the world you want to go, to disappear and begin a brand-new life. But I need you to be in this with me."

A tingling sensation crept up and down my spine. I had a feeling I knew what Ferrari had called me there for—what he'd arranged. But I didn't respond. I didn't say I was on board, yet I didn't say I wasn't. I actually had the nerve to not know what I wanted to do. I even thought for a second that what he had planned was the best outcome. I mean, for all of what his wife had done to him since he was just a teenager, maybe she deserved what he had up his sleeve . . . But wait a minute, what was I thinking? Who had I become to condone such a thing? Could I love Ferrari *that* much? I became frightened. I felt like I had made a big mistake. It was time for me to get back home, where I belonged.

## JuJu & Ferrari

"I'm back," JuJu sang dryly as she walked into the office of her friend, Private Investigator Mike Schwartz.

"And why so? You haven't figured out by now that the boy loves you?" the gray-haired, bespectacled man asked.

He stood up from behind his desk to greet JuJu with a hug and kiss on each cheek.

"Love has nothing to do with it," JuJu said, as she took a seat.

Mike sat back down. "What's going on?" He folded his hands under his chin.

"There's definitely someone else. And this time there's some real merit behind my suspicions."

"What would that be?"

JuJu took a deep breath and in a victim's pitch she explained, "I'm almost positive he's having sex with a woman behind my back. He texts a lot in the middle of the night while he thinks I'm asleep. And in the morning when I check his phone there are no messages during the hour that I saw him texting, so I know he's deleting them. And the straw that broke the camel's hump—"

"Back," Mike corrected her.

"What?"

"The saying goes, the straw that broke the camel's *back*, not hump," he clarified.

JuJu huffed with frustration. "Back, hump, it's all the same. The straw that broke it was that he didn't come home last night." JuJu's eyes narrowed with anger. "I think he's planning to leave me, to divorce me and take all of what I worked so hard for so that he and this girl can go off and live happily ever after on my dime. And I won't stand by idly while he plans his escape."

"Judith," Mike said, "do you think you're overreacting? Just a little bit? I mean, where is the evidence of all this?"

"That's what *you're* going to get," JuJu snapped. "I want you to track his conversations and his movements."

Mike shook his head. "I'm starting to think you have too much money to know what to do with."

"Trust me, I can think of a million better things to waste my money on than paying you to spy on my husband. I'm not here to spend my money. I'm here to *protect* my money."

"All right," Mike sighed and frowned, "I'll bill you."

"And why the pitiful face at getting paid to do what you get paid to do? Shouldn't it put a smile on your face to see me walk through that door?"

"You've been my friend for thirty years, Judith—though I'm never happy to see you walk through that door."

JuJu blushed, but very briefly, then stood up. "Well, anything you need from me, you let me know. Charge the card that's on file. And start today."

"Will do," Mike said, standing to walk her out of the office. "I'll have some preliminary information by the end of the week."

"Good." She kissed Mike on the cheek.

He opened the door for her and she walked out. He watched her get in her car, start it up, and back out of the parking space that might as well have had her name painted on it.

## Lyssa & Jacob

Jake and I were in Vegas for the annual Adult Entertainment Expo, the largest sex convention in the world. All the festivities were happening at the Hard Rock Hotel & Casino so we went through PanacheReport.com, a prestigious concierge company, to book a suite there plus VIP tickets to all the hottest parties and events coordinated with the convention. We hadn't been in two years so we went all out.

Opening and running the club kept us too busy for leisure vacations like this. But after the bombshell Morgan had dropped on us earlier that month, we could use the downtime. This was also the perfect opportunity to interview our new prospective live-in.

Jake found this one. He insisted on doing the research. He went on the site, scoped out all the options, and made all the calls. After prescreening four candidates, he found one who fit perfect with what we were looking for—single, no children, didn't smoke, drink or do any drugs, and was in school. We liked students because they seemed to have good heads on their shoulders. We stayed away from party animals because they drew too much attention to themselves and therefore to us.

Jake arranged for the girl to fly to Vegas and meet us at our hotel room the last day of the convention. If all went well at the interview, we would buy her a plane ticket to Atlanta and move her in with us within several weeks.

We slept in that last day. Attending close to one hundred presentations, trying to meet and greet about three hundred of the top adult stars in the business, watching

stage performances and musical acts and going to endless parties, left us exhausted. But we had a ball and did
a good deal of networking.

The concierge rang the hotel room phone at noon as I
had instructed them to do the night before. I answered
it.

"Good afternoon Mrs. Banner," the voice said, "this
is your wake-up call."

"Thank you," I muttered. Even at twelve in the afternoon I felt like it was too early for me to be getting up.
But I had to. Our new girl would be there at two.

"Jake," I shoved his arm a little, "wake up."

He hesitated.

"It's twelve o'clock. We still have to eat, get dressed,
and let the housekeeper come clean this room before she
gets here."

He turned on his back, stretched his arms above his
head, and opened his eyes. "I'm up," he groaned.

We ordered room service. While we waited for it to
come, we both showered. Jake was just about dressed by
the time the food arrived. I was still in the complimen-
tary robe applying my makeup.

We ate and watched world news. I took that time to
probe Jake more about this girl he had found all on his
own.

"So does she seem my type?"

"Yeah, from what I could tell."

"What do you mean, from what you could tell? Was she pretty or not?"

"She looked good to me," he said, stuffing his mouth.

"Let me see her picture." He didn't sound sure enough for me.

"What picture?" he asked, chewing. "The one on her profile?"

"No," I said, "those profile pics are always cropped at the neck. Didn't you ask her to e-mail you some additional pictures so you could actually see her face and not just her body?"

Jake almost choked on his food. He sipped his juice. "You do all that?" His face wrinkled with confusion.

"Of course!" I squealed.

"I just figured we'd see her in person and make our decision then."

I shook my head. *If you want something done right, you have to do it yourself,* I thought.

We had finished our food and were fully dressed by one. We killed time on the strip to give the housekeeper a chance to clean our room. It was perfect weather, not sweltering hot like Vegas was known for. That was the good thing about going during the winter months—it was comfortable.

Jake got a call at one-thirty. The girl was headed to our hotel from where she was staying by the airport.

"You gave her your cell number?" *Another mistake*, I thought.

"I know that you're not supposed to give your number. I had the hotel calls forwarded."

"Oh," I said, relieved, just slightly. We still had to see how this girl looked. If she was a turn-off, all of this would have been a sizable waste of time and money.

We got back to the room, freshened up a bit, and waited for the knock on the door. I was anxious, though Jake seemed pretty cool. But that was just how he was. Sometimes I questioned whether this was still fun for him.

*Knock knock knock.*

I looked at Jake. He looked back at me, a slight grin formed across his lips. He got up and walked to the door. Without even looking through the peephole, he opened it.

I was sitting on the couch against the same wall the door opened on. So from where I was, I could see the girl when Jake opened the door. And nothing could have prepared me for that sight.

"ALEXANDRIA?" I stood up.

"Ba-by?" Jake could hardly muster the words.

"Mommy, Daddy?" Our twenty-year-old daughter backed away shamefully.

"Get in here," I demanded, walking toward the door.

Jake was in shock. He just stood holding the door, his jaw on the floor. I was pissed.

She walked into our room, slowly. She was terrified. She had to have been. I was myself.

"What the hell are you doin' here?" I asked her.

"What are y'all doin' here?" she shot back, tears welling in her eyes.

I had to think of something quick. Under any other circumstances I wouldn't feel like I needed to explain myself to my daughter, but this was different. I had to offer up some sort of response.

"We heard you were doing this and we just couldn't believe it." I glanced over at Jake. He hadn't moved. "Jake, close the door." I didn't need the whole tenth floor hearing this dysfunctional conversation.

He let go of the door and joined me in the sitting area.

"We had to see for ourselves," I continued.

Alexandria sat down. She lowered her head. Tears flowed down her freshly powdered face. "I'm so sorry," she wept.

Jake looked at me. He put his hand over his mouth and shook his head. He was still in shock. As was I. Although we had managed to get ourselves out of the line of questioning and scrutiny, we had to deal with the fact that our own daughter was living a lifestyle we thought we had done a good job sheltering her from. The number one question I had was *why*.

"Just because," she said.

And I didn't expect any other answer. It couldn't have been for money; we paid her tuition and she wanted for nothing. It couldn't have been for housing; she had her own apartment on campus. And it sure wasn't out of desperation; she had always been a driven, strong-willed person. If she needed anything, she went and got it, and if anybody was trying to force her to do something she didn't want to do, she knew how to make him or her stop.

I couldn't help but ask myself if it was hereditary. Was the lifestyle something my husband and I just happened to enjoy or was it in our DNA?

## Danielle & Stewart

"It's up!" I rejoiced at launching the long-awaited video of the owner of Puss & Boots performing oral sex on me. Stew and I had been promoting the video for months. Our subscribers had been wanting to see if we could catch the boss of the place we operated out of on our hidden camera. They doubted we had the balls. And with the *Upload Complete* message that just shot across the computer screen, we showed them.

It was close to ten o'clock, time to head out to work. The *We Even Caught the Boss* video was the last of our ammunition. We needed to reload, and with Jake and Lyssa out of town for a convention we could have free reign over Puss & Boots.

The club was packed, as was typical for a Saturday. I saw some new faces and many old. I was on two pills so I was ready to go upon entering. But there was a protocol I had to follow, so instead of just joining in on the orgy that was taking place on one of the square, oversized, leather-topped daybeds, I headed straight for the bar.

Stew, from behind me, ordered our drinks. I scoped out our surroundings for a couple I felt could be interesting to our subscribers. I usually looked for people who were of course attractive, had pretty decent bodies, and who seemed like they would be a lot of fun or would transform behind the four walls of our room.

It was a hidden camera site so it wasn't like we could rely on acting from a set of characters. We needed people who were *natural* characters to make our videos entertaining. And one had just moved up next to me, eyeing me with a grin that could have made my panties come off—if I were wearing any.

She was an average-looking girl in the face but her body was enhanced in all the right places. Her breasts had to measure beyond a double-D. Her waist was thin, too thin for the huge behind that protruded from it. She couldn't have been born with that juicy thing. That had to be the result of butt shots.

I had always wanted to capture one of those for our site. With Nicki Minaj popularizing the enormous ass, I had wanted to offer that look to our viewership. I had always noticed it at the strip clubs in Atlanta but until that night I had never seen it walk through the doors of Puss & Boots. I was on it.

"Now *that's* an ass," I told her as she stood in the small space between the barstool I was sitting on and the empty one beside me.

"You like it?" she asked, locking her knees and shaking it effortlessly.

Stewart walked over to get a closer look, and I asked him for permission to touch it. He said, "Hell yeah."

First I rubbed it, then squeezed it, then gave it a light slap. The seductive grin and the licking of her own titties told me that she was enjoying herself. Stewart and I wouldn't need much talking or drinking to get her to our room. We went straight for the kill.

"You're coming with us," I told the girl. "Where's your guy?"

"I'm here with my *girl*," she countered, pointing at a table for two. "Is that cool?"

We followed her finger to an edgy-looking girl with half her head shaved and the other half overflowing with long silky purple hair. She was very light-skinned, though she wasn't white. Maybe Latina or biracial. She had piercings in her cheeks that created dimples. She was clearly a character.

"Sounds great," Stew said.

I nodded in agreement. This was going to be fun. The girl motioned for her friend to join us. We led them through the delirious crowd, and despite this being something I was far from new to, seeing so many random people openly having sex with other random people still had the affect on me it had my very first time. I couldn't turn away from it. I had to glance in the direction of every passionate scream and every orgasmic pant. And it always looked the same. Faces on the men told the story of intense pleasure, while faces on the women, of drunken excitement.

When we got inside our room, Stew locked the door and I removed my towel. The first girl pushed Stew down on the rotating bed, straddling him, her planet-sized bottom jiggling like Jell-O.

Her girlfriend with the purple hair then started peering around our room. "Where is it?" she asked, dragging her hands across the wall.

I smiled, half-crazed from the pills I had taken. "What are you talking about, sweetheart?" I walked up on her and reached out for her smaller but perky set of breasts.

She knocked my hand down. "Where's the camera?"

Stew tried to lift his head to see what was going on, but the girl on top of him was suddenly holding a tiny blade to his neck. It must've been under her tongue the whole time.

"Don't move another inch or you will lose your life tonight," she told Stew.

My smile quickly faded. Had we caught them on tape before and they were here for revenge? I pondered. But that could not have been the case, I thought, because I would have remembered the ass on that girl.

"We know y'all be secretly taping muthafuckas," Purple Hair said. "Now all we want is fifty G's and we'll walk outta here smiling like we had a good time. If not, we will shine the light on y'all lil' operation and I'm sure that'll cost y'all way more than what we askin'."

Extortion. I shoulda known. The eye contact and the ass shake at the bar were too strong a come-on even in a place like this. But fifty G's wasn't actually a lot to ask for. Stew and I had it, but did I want to part with it under these circumstances? Absolutely not. Extortionists got under my skin the way rapists and child molesters did. I wanted to tell her and her big-booty ho to bounce their thirsty asses out of my room and out of the club. But there was a blade to my husband's throat.

"Whose to say you won't cut us anyway after we hand over the money?" I asked.

"Whose to say we have that kind of money here?" Stewart talked over me.

"You keep quiet, old head," Big Butt told Stew.

Then Purple Hair summed it up: "Just like we know there's cameras in here, we know there's a stash in here. Now I can fuck all y'all shit up looking for it myself or you can hand it over peacefully and still have the chance to make it back with the next unsuspecting couple y'all lure back here."

"So what the fuck is it gonna be?" Big Butt shouted.

"Stew . . ." I began nervously.

"Give it to 'em," he surrendered. "Just give it to 'em so they can get the fuck outta here."

"Aye," Big Butt said, pressing the blade harder against his neck. "The aggression isn't necessary. It's not like we askin' for ya whole life's savings. We're being nice enough to leave ya business still intact."

"All right, all right, everybody calm down," I said, walking over to our stash spot behind one of the leather panels in the wall. I angrily counted out fifty thousand dollars, then closed the panel and turned to Purple Hair.

"Here," I handed her the stack of bills. "Now please just go." I was livid, definitely no longer high.

Purple Hair flipped through the money to make sure it was what she had asked for. "It's all here. Let's go," she told her girl.

"I'm gonna get up off you and you are not gonna make a move. The slightest motion and my girl will take *her* blade from out her mouth and make a real mess out ya pretty little wifey there, you got it?"

"Got it," Stew said.

And with that she slowly backed up off him. Meanwhile her girl would not take her eyes off me. I stood stiff, waiting for them to walk out and that be that.

Big Butt and Purple Hair backed their way over to the door, unlocked it, and walked out. As soon as the door shut behind them, I rushed over and locked it.

Stew jumped up and scrambled to another one of our stash spots. I was sure he was going for the gun.

"No," I stopped him. "If you run out there chasin' behind them with a gun, our cover will be blown."

"I don't give a fuck," Stew shot back. "These bitches just threatened my life and the life of my wife." He loaded the gun.

"It was just to get the money," I told him. "They weren't going to kill us. We overreact, we lose everything, just like that." I stood in front of him, looked him in his eyes. "I'm just as pissed as you are, believe me. But it's not like we were robbed making an honest living. We do to people what they just did to us except we don't use a weapon and the people we take from never find out they've been robbed of anything."

Stew eased up. His heavy breathing started to slow down.

"It's a drop of defeat in a bucket overflowing with victory," I concluded.

Stew let the clip out of the gun and put it back in our stash spot.

"From now on, no one comes in this room without being scanned by a metal detector. And first thing Monday, I'm having someone come through and outfit this place for guns. I want one under the bed, behind the TV, attached to the swing, everywhere. It just got real."

# CHAPTER 5

# NO APOLOGIES

## JuJu & Ferrari

THE TEMPERATURE DROPPED DRASTICALLY, from the low seventies earlier in the week to the low forties by the weekend. February wanted everybody to know she had arrived. JuJu was waiting beside her car in the parking lot of the yoga class she took every Saturday morning. Mike was meeting her there with some new information. She shook a little but it wasn't from the cold. Anxiety had set in.

Mike's car finally pulled up, and he stepped out carrying an orange envelope. She knew that meant pictures were inside. And Mike only brought pictures when there was something worth showing. A lump formed in her throat.

"Hi, hun," Mike greeted with a hug and kiss on each cheek like usual. She reciprocated.

"What did you find?" she got right to the point.

"Well," Mike said, pulling the envelope from under his arm, "you were right."

He handed JuJu a small stack of 5x7 black-and-white photographs. She examined the shots as he narrated.

"He had this young lady at the lake house on several occasions. The first was a couple days after you left my office. The last was last night."

"Son of a bitch," JuJu mumbled. "This is her." She looked up at Mike. "This is the girl I told you about."

"I know. And I put two and two together and found out that she's the same girl you suspected he'd been messaging on Facebook several months back."

JuJu's mouth flung open. "So you're telling me that he's been having an affair with her since back when I first hired you?"

Mike nodded and rubbed his hands together. "You wanna get out of this cold? Go grab some coffee?"

JuJu thought on it.

"I can tell you what he's planning," Mike added.

JuJu grimaced. "There's more?"

Mike nodded. "He booked a hotel room for Valentine's Day, and at first I thought maybe he's booking the room for the two of you. But that's not the case. Let's go somewhere and talk."

JuJu gave in. She needed to figure out her next move and Mike could help her do that. She had him follow her to Land of a Thousand Hills, her favorite coffee house in Atlanta.

During the fifteen-minute drive, JuJu wondered how she had let Ferrari get so far from her grasp. When did he grow the balls to do the things he was now doing. It was one thing for him to send inappropriate messages to a person on Facebook, but for him to actually invite the girl to their home, *her* home—that was a whole different level of disrespect and disregard. Then it dawned on her: if this same girl was the one he had been talking to on Facebook, then the night they met at Puss & Boots wasn't the first time they'd encountered one another like they had led everyone to believe. In fact, JuJu thought more into it, it couldn't have been a coincidence that Ferrari and this girl ended up at the same club that night. No one's luck was that good. They had to have planned it. JuJu grew more furious as she thought about just how conniving and underhanded Ferrari had been.

*I made him*, she told herself. *I took him from nothing. Everything he is, everything he has, is because of me! And I get repaid like this?*

Her intuition had turned out to be right. Her fears were legitimate. She was losing the control she had over her husband. Part of her felt like she should have expected this day would come sooner or later. She had met Ferrari when he was nineteen modeling in Los Angeles. She had taken one look at him and wanted him. She liked spoiling him and being in control in their relationship, and sex with somebody so many years her junior had started out thrilling.

But in the back of her mind, she always thought he'd get tired of being her possession. He would become a man one day and want a younger woman. That had always haunted her. That was why she could be so violent and threatening toward him. She thought those tactics would scare him into staying with her. It sure worked for her mother, who had managed to keep ahold on her father for thirty-plus years using a similar approach.

JuJu recalled times where she'd hear her mother, at the top of her lungs, hurling insults at her father. She'd lie at the top of the stairs and look down. She'd witness her mother hitting her father with household items like irons and toasters. She'd watch her threatening to electrocute him while he was bathing. All this and still her father remained married to her until his death. It was how you kept a man—or so JuJu grew up believing.

She was concerned now, though, that those very tactics might have been what was driving Ferrari into the arms of this girl. He was probably at the point of no return, where he felt he had nothing left to lose, so fear no longer drove him—desperation did.

# Tori & Kevin

I had just walked in from another overnight stay with Ferrari at the lake house. It was becoming a pattern much like our conversing back and forth over the Internet where this whole thing began. I kept telling myself it was going to be the last time, but something kept pulling me back. I ended up blaming it all on fate. It was my way of justifying my actions. *Maybe it's meant to be,* I often told myself, *maybe it's God's plan.*

It was ten a.m. Typically Kevin would be at the gym at this hour. It was his Saturday-morning routine. That would have given me the chance to shower, organize my thoughts, and deplete my guilt so that I wouldn't come off as sneaky or guarded by the time Kevin got home.

But that morning Kevin didn't go to the gym. He was just getting out of the shower when I got to our bedroom. I was caught off guard, but I tried to carry myself as normal as possible.

"Hey," I greeted.

"What's up?" he replied, drying his hair in the mirror.

"You goin' somewhere?" He didn't tend to shower before the gym.

"Yeah." He brushed past me, his eyes avoiding contact with mine.

I put my pocketbook in the closet and took off my sneakers. I always dressed down when I went to see Ferrari. I didn't want to raise any red flags by fixing myself up to go "help my mother out."

"My mom is doing better," I volunteered.

"Oh yeah?" He rushed his clothes on.

"Everything okay?" I had to ask. Kevin was throwing me too much shade.

"Yup," he said flatly.

"Where are you going?"

"I gotta meet somebody real quick."

"Who? Where?" I removed my sin-covered clothing.

"A friend. At the Land of a Thousand Hills."

"The coffee spot?" I was confused. Kevin wasn't a coffee drinker.

"She picked the spot, not me," he said nonchalantly as he tied his sneakers.

"She?"

He pretended not to hear me and left the room. I hurried behind him, naked and all.

"Who the hell is *she?*" I yelled at his back as he jogged down the stairs.

Kevin was no longer pretending. He was outright ignoring me. I ran down the stairs behind him.

"Who are you meeting, Kevin?"

He grabbed the car keys off the wooden peg that

hung on the wall in the hallway leading to our two-car garage.

I followed him to the door, but no further. I couldn't risk the neighbors seeing me in the nude.

"Kevin!" I shrilled.

He opened the car door.

"KEVIN!"

He didn't respond, he simply started the car and backed out of the garage. The screeching of the tires was like an exclamation point on the end of his silent anger.

He knew something. What and how, I had yet to find out.

## Lyssa & Jacob

Boy how I wished the expression *What happens in Vegas stays in Vegas* was true. I wished Jake and I were able to leave the shocking revelation we had discovered back there out west. There was no way, though. I was still suffering from unanswered questions.

And as soon as we got back home to Atlanta, we sought out a family therapist. Jake and I had no idea how to deal with our daughter's desires and choices. We felt like hypocrites every time we tried talking to her about it. The end result was that all of us had to come clean. It was hard as hell. But it had to be done for us to open up the lines of communication.

We finally confessed to Alexandria that it wasn't an assisted living home we invested our retirement money in, but a swingers club. And that we had in fact called her out to Vegas not to bust her but to interview her. It was what we were into.

In turn, she admitted that she began working as a bartender at a strip club after her first semester in college. She said that had progressed to dancing. And she had experimented with being a live-in for a couple near her campus that same summer. It was purely for fun and an additional source of easy income.

The information was difficult to digest. For her as well, I could imagine. But at least by the time Alexandria left to return to school, we were all understanding one another. It was awkward to be in each other's presence, yes, but we only saw each other during holidays and summers, so it wouldn't be too bad.

We promised to keep our admissions between the three of us. Not to let it get out to our extended family and especially not to Jake Jr., Alexandria's older brother. He was heavily grounded in the church and we were all sure our secrets were too seedy for him to handle. He was likely to disown us all if he found out.

Jake and I went back to work running Puss & Boots as if nothing had happened. We did however put trying to find another live-in on hold. It was hard to screen girls, interview them, and even think about bringing them into our bed without thinking they could be our daughter. So when Morgan called the club asking if she could come back to work for us, I was prepared to decline. But I was also curious.

"What about the baby?" I asked her through the phone.

"There was never a baby," she huffed.

"What do you mean?"

"I was never pregnant, Lyssa. Please don't get mad, but Jacob wanted me to tell you that. He said he thought you were getting too clingy with me. He didn't want to cause any problems in y'all's marriage. I wanna respect his wishes, but I ran outta money. I need a place to stay. And . . ." she rambled on.

I could not believe what I was hearing, but it made sense. That was the reason Jake had wanted to choose our next live-in. He wanted to pick somebody he felt I wouldn't be so drawn to. Well, the joke was on him. Not only did he pull the wrong card, our daughter, but now he was going to have to deal with Morgan, 'cause I was moving her back in.

# Danielle & Stewart

Stewart and I were driving to the gun range where we had an appointment to get some weapons training. Ever since the robbery, extortion, or whatever you choose to call it, Stew has been getting us ready for war. But in the process of all of the preparation for another incident, I started having doubts. How was I to ever relax and let myself go thinking about the possibility of somebody robbing us at knifepoint or gunpoint. How much money were we willing to lose, and more importantly, what if the next time the knife actually gets used?

I was beginning to think twice about the whole idea. Then I realized I was ready to do what we always did when the tides changed in our business—relocate.

"You know what I was thinking?" I began.

"What?" Stew asked, eyes on the road.

"How about we just move again?"

"What are you talking about?" He glanced over at me.

"All this outfitting the room for guns and getting weapons training is scary, Stew, and ready or not, I don't want to have to even worry about needing all this stuff, not in a place where I'm supposed to be completely at ease and carefree. How can I work the same with the threat of someone sticking us up hanging over my head? It's never going to be like it was before."

Stew nodded. "I've been thinking the same thing, actually. Our safety has been jeopardized and we can arm ourselves to the teeth, but it will never be the same."

"I say we look at the top three places we'd want to go. Book us some flights and spend a couple weeks checking them out. We come back in time for the event at the club. Make a good amount of videos that night to last us until we get situated in our new place, then we leave Atlanta as just another marked territory."

"Sounds like a plan," Stewart said, making an abrupt U-turn. "Call and cancel the weapons appointment and look up flights to Vegas, Phoenix, and maybe even Dallas since that cowboy brought us in so many new subscribers."

I got on my phone and did just that. There was something special about starting fresh. Going to a new territory where nobody knew nor could suspect what you had or who you were gave me a new sense of security.

# CHAPTER 6

## SUNGLASSES AND ADVIL

### JuJu & Ferrari

JUJU NERVOUSLY SIPPED AWAY AT HER THIRD CUP OF HAITIAN BLEND. Her eyes peered out the window, but instead of taking in the beauty of the Chattahoochee River, she was watching every person who approached the front door, anxiously awaiting Kevin.

After Mike disclosed all of what he had discovered about Ferrari and Tori, JuJu's wheels got to turning. She wanted to figure out a clever way to bust Ferrari that would leave him unable to make excuses and unable to get one red cent from a divorce settlement. She had come up with a plan and called Kevin.

After an hour or so, she finally spotted him walking through the door. She stood up and waved him over. The last time she had seen him she was giving him fellatio. The memory shot through her mind as she hugged him hello.

"Thanks for coming all the way out here," JuJu said as she and Kevin sat.

"Oh, no problem. It was only about a thirty-minute drive for me."

"You're by the Mall of Georgia, right?"

"Lawrenceville, yeah."

"That's a hell of a ways for a girl to go every other day for some penis . . . No offense."

"None taken."

"Did your wife stay out last night?"

Kevin nodded.

JuJu stirred her coffee. "Yeah, he did too. This time, though, it wasn't that he stayed out with an old friend who had come into town and lost track of the time. It was fishing with friends and somehow he had too much to drink to drive home. Slept on their sofa until he sobered up," she sneered.

"Tori's excuse is always her mom. She was recently declared legally blind and so Tori would go help her around the house on certain weekends, but now it's almost every weekend and even some days during the week."

"Yeah, well . . ." JuJu sipped her coffee, then pulled some pictures from her tote bag. "The PI I hired took these."

Kevin skimmed through them. His eyes watered as he looked at still shots of his wife in another man's arms. He gave the pictures back to JuJu and rubbed his hands over his face.

"I didn't think it was fair for either of us to be in the dark about this," JuJu explained, "especially after finding out that it's been going on for so long."

"Yeah, since November." Kevin shook his head in disbelief.

JuJu looked up at him sorrowfully. "No, since *well* before November."

"What do you mean since before November? That night we met at the club was the first time Tori had ever seen your husband."

"I thought that too," JuJu said. "But do you recall ever catching your wife sending messages to someone on Facebook or texting in the middle of the night?"

Kevin immediately thought back to a time about five months into their marriage when he was woken out of his sleep by a buzzing coming from Tori's phone. Plugged into the charging station on his side of the bed, he couldn't help but glance down at it. It was a text. Who was texting his wife at two in the morning? He reached down to take the phone off the charger. But before doing so, he looked over at his wife. She was sleeping like a baby.

He picked up the phone and read the text message, which had come from a number that wasn't saved in Tori's phone. It read: *I need to talk. Are you up?*

Kevin was alarmed. He started to write back but he

looked over at his wife again and realized that the typing might wake her. So he got out of bed and moved into the bathroom.

*What's wrong?* he typed back.

*Where were you today? Why did you stand me up?*

Kevin stared at the message before typing a reply. *This can't be happening*, he thought to himself. *We're new- lyweds. She can't be cheating on me already*. He was hurt, but a little thankful that Tori hadn't met up with the person texting her phone. Maybe her love for Kevin was what kept her from meeting the person. Maybe she was loyal to him. He took that into consideration and decided to protect his marriage.

*This is Tori's husband. You let this be the last time you contact her in any way*, Kevin typed, then pressed *Send*. But he had more to say. *If I find out you reached out to her or tried to see her after today, I will track you down and make you regret you ever fell for my wife.*

Kevin deleted all the messages, put the phone on the charger, and climbed back in bed next to his wife. He hugged her and kissed her all over her face.

"Don't ever hurt me," he whispered in her ear. "Please. I love you so much."

"I won't," she whispered back in her sleep. "I love you too."

Kevin took comfort in that and held onto the belief

that that was where any possibility of an affair between Tori and another man had started and stopped. He let it go.

Bringing himself out of his memory and back into the present, he looked at JuJu. "Yes," he nodded, "I do remember one time some random number texted her in the wee hours of the morning."

"It was my husband, I bet. He and your wife have been communicating through Facebook and text messages for some time now. I've caught him on several occasions. The thing is, I never saw her face. The Facebook profile she made to communicate with him was private and it had no picture, so when we met you all at Puss & Boots that night I had no idea that your wife was the same girl he had been communicating with for almost a year."

"Almost a year?" Kevin was taken aback. He had put Tori on a pedestal. Always believed she was angelic. And even when that suspicious text came through he wrote it off as a one-time mistake. "So you're saying they knew each other before that night at the club?"

"Yes, and I'm willing to bet the ranch that they planned to meet there. A way for them to get away with sleeping together. Right up under our noses. That's why I called you here. It's been going on too long and it's gotten too deep."

Kevin's eyes watered again and this time the levy broke. He turned his face, trying to hide the tears from JuJu. But there was no hiding his sobs.

JuJu grabbed a couple of napkins off the small stack beside her cup and handed them to Kevin.

He took them and held them in his hand for several moments. He dropped his head. Drowning in self-pity, he said, "I'm sorry." He wiped his eyes with one of the napkins and regained eye contact with JuJu. "My wife is all I got. Her and her mom and her dad were all the family I have ever known. I don't have a family myself. I don't have many friends. Her friends are my friends. Without her I have nobody. I can't lose her." He shook his head again. "If I lose her, I'll have nothing, I'll have no one. I'll have absolutely nothing to live for." His sobbing dulled down to a whimper and he used the rest of the napkins to completely dry away his tears. At that point Kevin's body language shifted. Where he had been worried, hurt, now he was disgusted, devastated. He couldn't be still.

"I hope you're not upset with me."

"I'm not upset at you, no. I'm upset at her and at him," he assured her.

JuJu reached her hand across the table and put it on top of Kevin's. She tried to calm his shaking. "I know you want to confront her about this and I want to do the same, but I think it would be best if we did it together, when we are all in the same room. This way, neither of them will be able to feed us bullshit."

"Unless you can get us all in the same room together within the next twenty minutes, I don't see how that's going to work," Kevin said angrily.

JuJu picked up her phone and scrolled to a text message from Mike. She showed it to Kevin. "Just like I had my guy following my husband, I had him tracking his phone calls and text messages. And Ferrari called the Marriott Marquis and reserved a room on the fourteenth . . ."

"Valentine's Day?"

JuJu nodded.

"So you expect me to wait damn near two weeks to address something like this?"

"I know it sounds impossible, it feels unbearable. I am in the same position, my friend. But we have to play this smart or else it could just end up being a denial party that starts from now until . . ."

"Wow." Kevin couldn't find any other words to describe how he felt. "This is crazy."

"I say we meet them at the hotel. We show up right after they do. There will be no talking their way out of that."

"Honestly," Kevin said, giving JuJu her phone back, "I cannot bite my tongue for that long. There's no way."

"I understand, but if we confront them now, they won't go to the hotel and I won't catch him red-handed."

"How much more red do you need his hands to be? What you just revealed to me is enough, isn't it?"

"Not in a court of law. I'm worth millions of dollars. If I divorce Ferrari, he'll get half of everything. Him hugging a woman in a picture won't stop that. But," JuJu raised her finger, "if I catch him in a hotel room having sex with that woman, that clause in our prenuptials will be deemed null and void."

Kevin took a deep breath. He thought about what JuJu was asking him to do. He wanted to help her, especially since she was the one making him aware of what was really going on. "Okay, I'll wait," he said reluctantly.

"Thank you!" JuJu put the pictures back in her bag and retrieved her checkbook in the same motion. "I'm going to write you a check for one hundred thousand dollars."

Kevin shook his head. "No, that won't be necessary." He had already made up his mind. A bribe wouldn't do.

JuJu looked at him. "You may be called in to testify if this thing gets ugly. You'll be the only other eyewitness who can corroborate my side of the story. You'll be the key to me holding onto my fortune. And for that, a hundred grand is the least I can do."

Kevin felt better about accepting the check after that pep talk. Leaving the quaint little coffee house, he had mixed emotions. On one hand, he felt like he had just won the lottery. On the other, he felt like he had just lost a piece of himself.

JuJu drank the rest of her coffee, then got up and left, saying goodbye to the employees of the place who all knew her. Her plan was in motion, that part she felt good about, but it involved losing her companion of eleven years in a week and five days. There was no solace in that.

## Lyssa & Jacob

I had just hung up the phone with Morgan, but before I could call Jake and give him the cursing out of a lifetime, a customer walked in with a chip on his shoulder.

I watched from inside my office as Kelsey greeted the small pale guy.

"Where is the owner or manager of this place?" I could hear him faintly through the thick glass of my office window.

Kelsey knocked on the door.

"Come in," I raised my voice.

Kelsey started to tell me what I already knew. The guy wanted to speak with me. I walked out of my office to the front entrance of the club.

"How can I help you?" I braced myself.

"I need you to tell me how my partner and I ended up on a porn site after coming here to your club!" he demanded. "What kind of business are you running here where you would secretly record people while they are at their most vulnerable?"

Of all the complaints I could have gotten, I didn't see that one coming. I had to take a moment to compose myself.

"First things first," I began. "We don't record anybody in this establishment with or without their permission and especially not without. So maybe you have the wrong club."

"I have the right club. In fact, the couple we were filmed with, they have some kind of VIP status with you. They get special treatment and they have their own private room . . ."

Instantly a lightbulb went off in my head. "Wait a minute, are you talking about Danielle and Stewart?"

I saw Kelsey nod in my peripheral.

The gentleman corrected me: "Mrs. Oxford and her husband."

"Do you have that video?" I asked.

"I have the link. And there are people threatening to put it in the wrong hands," he said, fear in his voice.

"Would you mind stepping into my office?"

The man shook his head and followed me into my office.

I turned on my laptop. "Have a seat," I gestured to a second chair next to the computer screen. "Pull up the link, please."

He did, first having to sift through e-mail messages to get to it. When he opened it and a porn site popped up with membership fees, advertisements, and everything, I was at a loss for words. *So this is how they make all their money*, I thought. *He plays football overseas my ass. No wonder they put so much money into that room—it was a business expense.*

"I had no idea I was being filmed," the man disrupted my thoughts. "I'm a mayoral candidate in my hometown in Texas, and now I'm being blackmailed because of this." The words quivered off his thin lips.

I took a breath. I had to somehow deal with this. "Okay, so when were you and your wife here? When did this happen?"

"That's the other problem," he said. "She's not my wife."

"Do you have a wife?" I hoped he would say no.

"Yes, and four kids."

"Shit."

"I just need this to come down off this site immediately!"

"I can assure you that I will have it taken down, but the couple responsible for this just left town today."

"Well, can you get them on the phone, e-mail, or something? This could destroy everything—my marriage, my career . . ."

"I can try." I picked up my cell and called Danielle's number. It went straight to voicemail. Same thing happened when I called Stewart. I didn't have an e-mail address for either of them, so all I could do was wait for them to return my calls or come walking through the door. "I'm sorry. Both of their phones are off, but I do know they'll be back on Valentine's Day. They're hosting an event here."

The man looked hopeless. "Okay, I'll come back then."

"If I reach them beforehand, I will make them take the site down, believe me. This goes against our policies in the worst way."

The man left, defeated. I immediately sat down in front of the computer. I needed to see who else had fallen victim to Danielle and Stewart's scam. And more importantly, had I?

## Danielle & Stewart

When we landed at Phoenix's Sky Harbor International Airport it was six in the evening. Stewart and I had both missed calls from Lyssa. We were concerned. Lyssa hardly ever called us, there was never a need. We saw each other at the club and talked about everything in person. So what could she possibly want that was important enough to call not one but both of us? My thoughts immediately traveled to the possibility that the girls had come back to Puss & Boots looking to get more money out of us. It was what extortionists did. They bled you dry.

"Did you check your voicemail?" I asked my husband as we sat on the plane waiting for it to taxi to our gate. A message would at least give us a hint as to what was going on.

"I checked. She didn't leave a message."

"She didn't leave one on mine either."

"Well, it must not be that important," Stew said.

I figured he had to be right. If someone came in there threatening to slice throats, Lyssa would have left a message. I was relieved, but more so because we had decided to make a move. The nervousness and anxiety behind getting missed calls from Lyssa was further proof that we were making the right decision by leaving Atlanta.

"Should we call her back?" I asked my husband.

He shook his head, "Nah, we'll see what she wants

when we get back to town. If it's a problem, well, we'll just leave right away. If it's not, we'll stick to our plan—collect us some videos to keep our subscribers entertained while we settle in and recycle our business plan."

I trusted Stew's wisdom and his instincts. They had managed to keep us on the right side of things for years now. I wasn't going to go against them now.

I turned my phone back off and patiently waited to get to the gate. I anticipated seeing what kind of swingers clubs Arizona had to offer and hoped we would find one that made us feel at home again. I was sure going to miss Puss & Boots. But change was ironically the only constant in our line of work so we were simply doing what we did.

## Tori & Kevin

My alarm buzzed at six forty-five as it did every weekday morning. Usually Kevin would put it on snooze for me so I could get another ten minutes of sleep. But he wasn't in the bed. He had slept in the guest bedroom where he had spent every night since he stormed out of here to meet some female at a coffee spot.

He wouldn't tell me what I had done to piss him off, but he didn't have to. I knew what I was doing, and whether he knew or not, I deserved the treatment he was giving me. It felt like karma.

So I dealt with it. I dealt with him not speaking to me. I dealt with him distancing himself from me. Selfishly, I used it as an excuse to continue my bad behavior. In fact, that very day, Valentine's Day, I had agreed to leave work a little early and meet Ferrari at a hotel downtown. He said he had a surprise for me. I planned to spend a couple hours with him and get back home the same time I would have if I left work at my regular time. That way Kevin wouldn't suspect a thing. And plus, Kevin and I would still make the party that evening at Puss & Boots. Lyssa and Jacob were using the event to raise money for a cause they supported every year around this time, the only reason Kevin was still willing to go with me.

I rose, got washed and dressed, brushed my teeth, did my hair and makeup, and headed downstairs. Kevin was still in bed for some reason. I could usually hear him moving about by the time I made it down to the kitchen to grab a light breakfast. But not that day. Maybe he overslept or wasn't feeling well. I decided to check on him.

I went back upstairs and crept toward the guest bedroom in the middle of the hall. I tapped on the door, then opened it. Kevin was knocked out, laid across the bed in the clothes he had worn the day before, snoring and all. That was unusual. I tiptoed up to him. That's when I smelled the liquor. It seemed like it was seeping from his pores. He must have gone out late last night. Probably had a hangover. I covered him up and left the room, then called his boss and told him Kevin was too sick to come in to work. He could thank me later.

I returned to the kitchen, grabbed a granola bar out of the pantry and a bottled water out of the refrigerator. As I left the house a dark cloud of shame hovered over me. What I was doing to Kevin was destroying him and deteriorating our marriage. Today would be my last day being with Ferrari. I meant it for real this time. I felt it in my heart. I believed it in my mind. This was it.

# CHAPTER 7

## LOVE IS CURSED BY MONOGAMY

### JuJu & Ferrari

JUJU WAS ALL OVER THE PLACE. She didn't think she would be so nervous. It was the afternoon of Valentine's Day, a holiday rooted in love. But she was filled with so much hate. Up to the very last minute, she wanted bad to confront Ferrari about his plans that afternoon. Especially because of how normal he was acting throughout the day.

He worked out with her that morning. He ate breakfast with her, even laughed at a couple of her jokes. He told her he was going out to buy her a gift and that he would be back in time for them to go to the Cupid event at Puss & Boots. He even hugged and kissed her before he left. It took everything in her not to ring his neck.

It was two thirty. Check-in was at three and that was also the time Ferrari had texted Tori to meet him at the hotel. *Rotten bastard,* JuJu thought.

She threw on some clothes in a rage. Her heart beat

rapidly. She waited on edge for about twenty minutes before she left her home. She and Kevin had planned to meet at the hotel at four to give Ferrari and Tori time to get in and settled.

She left her condo, speed-walked down the hall, and took the elevator to the parking garage. She was already in her car with the engine running when she realized she had left her phone in the house. She contemplated going back up and getting it. She looked at the time. She had five minutes to spare, so she turned the car off and darted back into the building.

She took the elevator back up to her unit, the penthouse suite. Upon exiting the elevator she could hear her phone ringing. She hurried to get it but had just missed a call from Mike. She listened to the message as she walked from her bedroom back to her front door.

*"Judith, it's me, Mike."* The urgency in Mike's voice immediately concerned her. *"Listen, if you're home, leave now. Go to a public place. I intercepted more of Ferrari's texts. He didn't send that 'I'm ready' text to the girl. He sent it to a guy. I don't know how to tell you this, but he put a hit out on you . . ."*

JuJu's heart sank. She gasped. Then she dropped her phone. She felt rough hands on her neck. A big guy in a ski mask was suddenly choking the life out of her. She tried ripping his hands away, but her strength was no match for him. Her eyelids began to flutter. She was losing consciousness. Her phone started ringing again. She tried using her feet to possibly answer the phone with hopes the person on the other end would hear her gasping for air. But her feet were no longer even touching the floor.

She was being attacked and her husband, the man who had orchestrated it, was off making love to another woman. Juju's terror evaporated as she collapsed in her killer's grip.

## Tori & Kevin

"Where are you, JuJu?" Kevin muttered under his breath as he sat in his car in the Marriott parking lot. He looked at the time on his cell phone. It was after four. He had waited in pain long enough to confront Tori, and JuJu being late could cause him to miss his opportunity. His head pounded with a headache from his all-night drinking binge.

He dialed her number.

*"You've reached a supermodel, baby, lucky you. Leave a message and please be detailed—"*

He hung up in the middle of her message. *I'll give her five more minutes*, he told himself.

He got out of his car in four. He locked it up and

headed to the hotel entrance. At the front desk, he did as JuJu had directed: he told the woman he had locked himself out of his room and needed another key.

"What's your room number?"

"817."

"Mr. Ferrari Ribeiro?"

"Yes," Kevin nodded.

The clerk dug in her stash of magnetic keys and handed one to Kevin. "Enjoy your evening Mr. Ribeiro."

JuJu was right. It was so busy on Valentine's Day the clerks couldn't remember every face that checked in and out.

Kevin took the elevator to the eighth floor, growing more discontented with every stop. He followed the signs to room 817. When he put his ear to the door, the sounds he heard made him want to kill somebody.

## Lyssa & Jacob

From the amount of RSVPs, we were expecting a big turn-out at the club that night. We had it fully catered and the bars were well stocked. We had extra staff on hand too. I was looking forward to us all having a good time. I even invited Morgan.

Jacob didn't know yet. He didn't even know that we

had spoken. The whole ordeal with Danielle and Stewart running a porn site from our club had occupied all of our conversations since I found out about it. We had spoken to our attorney about our options, and since we had not only been defrauded by Danielle and Stewart using our club to conduct their business, but I was also a victim of them illegally recording me, we had a lawsuit on our hands.

Come to find out, Danielle was trying to get me to have sex with her at the club just so she could tape me. And when that didn't work, she had set up a camera at her house and taped me at their Christmas party. That helped our case, though, because had all the recordings been at the club, Danielle and Stewart could have argued that Jake and I had given them permission to set up the video recorder. They could have lied and said the additional membership fees they paid were our cut of the profits they made off the site. But seeing as they had me on tape at their home, and the fact that they captioned the video *We Even Caught the Boss,* we had a solid case that we were not in on the scheme.

We hadn't spoken to Danielle and Stewart about any of it. They hadn't returned our calls. We didn't want to leave a message and scare them off, so we just waited for them to get back to town and figured we'd catch up with them at our event they agreed to host.

I was instructing the party planners I'd hired on where to put the furniture and decor when I heard Kelsey's voice squeal, "Mor-gan!"

I couldn't lie, just hearing her name made my vagina throb. I excused myself from the party planners and headed out to the front entrance.

As soon as our eyes met, Morgan ran into my arms. I hugged her tight and we immediately began kissing. It was throbbing double-time now.

"I missed you so much," I told her, not wanting to let her go.

"Awww, get a room," Kelsey teased.

Morgan giggled like a schoolgirl. "I missed you too," she said, gently wiping the residue from her lipstick off my mouth.

"I haven't told Jake yet," I said, finally releasing her.

Her face froze.

"But he kept a secret from me, so I can keep one from him," I explained.

Morgan relaxed.

"Payback is a bitch," I said, "with some good-ass pussy."

# CHAPTER 8

# THE PAIN AIN'T CHEAP

## Tori & Kevin

FERRARI AND I WERE ENGROSSED IN A THREESOME. A girl he knew had agreed to be my Valentine's Day surprise from him. She was very pretty, and exotic like him. They were both natives of Brazil. My thighs were propped on her shoulders while she sucked the natural juices from my peach. It was a nickname she had given me based on me being a Georgia girl.

My back was leaned against the headboard. I was sitting upright, my eyes following Ferrari as he slid out of her and walked over to the side of the bed. He climbed up on it, planting his feet as firmly as he could on the soft mattress. He positioned his body sideways, facing me, gripped my head in his hands, and put his dick in my mouth.

I could taste remnants of her—he wasn't wearing a condom. I didn't care though. I liked being naughty. It turned me on. It was one of the reasons I found it so hard to be faithful to Kevin. But this was it, I still intended to keep my promise to myself that this would be our last hoorah.

Ferrari pumped my mouth vigorously. He was feeling good too. I could tell because when the hotel room door opened up and Kevin appeared before us, he didn't stop. He simply kept pumping.

What happened next was a blur. I remember Kevin charging at Ferrari. The girl was struck with fear as she threw her clothes on and got out of there with lightning speed. I tried to break Kevin and Ferrari apart, but it was no use. Kevin was in as great shape as Ferrari. There was nothing I could do to pull them off each other.

"I told you to end all contact with my wife!" Kevin yelled as he wrapped his hands around Ferrari's neck.

"Stop!" I screamed at Kevin. "You're going to kill him!"

Kevin ignored my pleas. He was focused only on Ferrari, who seemed to be slipping in and out of consciousness. "I warned you," he told Ferrari through clenched teeth. "I told you I would make you regret it! And you didn't stop. You even had the nerve to set up that trip to Puss & Boots so that you could have sex with my wife right in front of me, knowing that I had texted you and told you to stay away from her, knowing that I had warned you what I would do if you reached out to her again. YOU THOUGHT I WAS JOKING? YOU THOUGHT YOU'D MAKE ME OUT TO BE A LIAR?" Kevin's rage was unlike anything I had seen before.

I knew if I didn't do something, Kevin would regret this for the rest of his life. I jumped on his back, trying to pull him off Ferrari or at least convince him to let go. I tried to the bitter end. But by the time Kevin had swung me off, it was too late. Ferrari was lifeless.

His body was curled up in the corner between the bed and window. Kevin's handprints were engraved in his neck. I broke out in tears, my body shook with fear.

"Call the police," I told Kevin, who was leaned up against the bed, breathless, staring at Ferrari in disbelief. "Call the police!"

Kevin didn't go for the phone. Instead he charged at Ferrari again, but this time to give him CPR. He blew breath into Ferrari's mouth, pounded on his chest, listened for any sign of life, and repeated the steps all over again.

I ran for the phone and started to dial 911.

"Wait," Kevin said. Panic seemed to set in. He stood up. He paced the small room. He rubbed his mouth and goatee. He shed tears.

"We have to call the police. They may be able to save him," I cried, the phone quivering in my hand.

"He's dead, there's no saving him," Kevin said. "We can't call the police."

"What do you mean? We have to."

Kevin stood in front of me and held my arms down by my side. "Tori, I will go to jail for the rest of my life and that will be on your hands. That over there," he pointed at Ferrari, "that's on your hands." He was trying to convince me not to involve the authorities. His words poked away at me like darts aiming for the bull's eye. They stuck but didn't hit the mark until . . . "You want your mom's last memories of her only child to be of her frequenting a swingers club, having a threesome with a married man and some strange girl, causing her son-in-law to throw his life away all because he loved her daughter too much?"

Bull's eye.

The thought of my mom listening to this story unfold on every news channel made me think twice about calling the police. The fact that Kevin was right—this was all my fault—also made me pause. I had truly messed up. And having lost Ferrari, I didn't want to lose Kevin too. Besides, I had obviously put him through enough. And he had done nothing but be a great husband, partner, and friend to me. The guilt I felt deemed the death penalty. I released the phone, letting it fall into Kevin's palm. He put it in his pocket and wiped his eyes.

"Get yourself together," he said, rubbing my arms as I let them hang down by my sides. "Get dressed . . . quick." He threw my clothes at me.

I did what I was told, too numb to think on my own.

"This never happened," Kevin murmured as he dragged Ferrari's body to the closet. "You hear me?"

I didn't answer. I was still crying and shaking, trying to put my clothes on.

"This never happened! All right?"

I nodded, sniffling, trying to control my tears.

"He got this room for the night, so nobody will come in here until tomorrow around check-out," Kevin seemed to be thinking aloud. "We'll hide him in here," he said, opening the closet. "Early in the morning, before the sun comes up, we'll take him out of here." He struggled to fit Ferrari's muscular six-foot frame inside.

"Can't we tell them it was an accident?" I searched for one more out to call the police before I would totally commit to becoming an accessory to murder.

"An accident is when somebody falls and hits their head or a gun goes off during a fight. There's no way to classify choking somebody to death as an accident."

"It was a crime of passion," I suggested. "People use that defense all the time and get off."

"And just as many people don't get off," Kevin mumbled as he closed the closet door. Then he dropped forward, letting his hands rest on his knees, and cried.

In time, I joined him and we wept together. I had realized that Kevin was probably right. Nothing could justify what he had done. If the police got involved, he would go to jail for murder. I had to help him. I couldn't live with myself being responsible for two people losing their lives.

"What are we going to do?"

Kevin wiped his face and stood up. He thought for a second. "We're gonna go to the club—"

"I can't go to the club after this."

"You RSVP'd, didn't you?"

I nodded. "Yeah, but . . ."

"If we don't show up, we have no alibi and we look suspicious," he explained. "We have to carry on like normal. We'll return here with a suitcase and remove the body. When they come in to clean the room, they'll think he checked out."

I went along with Kevin's plan and it killed me inside that what I had done led to all of this. How I would manage to act normal later on at Puss & Boots, I didn't know—until I got there. I ordered drink after drink. I didn't leave the bar. I was trying to drown away the horrors of the day. Even when I felt the intense need to urinate, I stayed glued to the barstool. Kevin was beside me, but he wasn't drinking as much. In fact, he wasn't drinking at all.

Danielle and Stewart were in the center of the dance floor putting on a live show. Everybody was gathered around watching them. Two girls sandwiched Danielle to form a pyramid. Stewart took turns dipping in and out of each of them. The entire club was entranced by their act when two uniformed police officers walked in.

No words can describe the terror and overwhelming grief I felt in the pit of my stomach.

## Danielle & Stewart

I was rolling, high off a pill and about three shots. The slightest touch sent shockwaves through me. I was relishing the pleasures of my husband and our two volunteers and even more so the audience we commanded. I moaned dramatically. I loved the spotlight. I loved sex. And I was enjoying both at the same time. If only we could manage to get this on tape, I thought with a laugh.

My husband had just taken his pipe out of me and put it in the top girl. I could feel him pounding her on my back since she was positioned on top of me. Her screaming in delight right above me had me yearning for more. I started rubbing my kitty cat against the bottom girl's butt cheek, seeking some relief. And to be sure she was being pleased too, I let my fingers find their way down to her midsection. Her hand was already there, though, rubbing forcefully like a deejay scratching a record. That pace could only mean one thing: she was on her way to an orgasm. And she was a squirter too, so that was bound to be a sight for our audience, who had grown eerily quiet by that time. I imagined it was anticipation of the volcanic eruption that was about to burst from the bottom girl.

But when I felt a hand on my shoulder and turned around to see two figures in dark uniforms, I understood the audience's silence. Before I could react, I heard my name—my real name—and I became a lot more aware.

"Christine Fisher," the officer's voice sobered me.

My husband backed out of the top girl, his face wrinkled with confusion. "What the hell is goin' on?" he asked.

"Mr. Fisher," the officer said, as he moved to place Stew's wrists in cuffs, "you and your wife Christine are under arrest for the illegal installation, placement, or use of a device for observing, recording, transmitting, photographing, or eavesdropping in a private place."

The other officer cuffed me. "You have the right to remain silent, whatever you say can and will be used against you in a court of law, you have the right to an attorney . . ."

I exercised my rights and kept quiet. There was nothing I could say anyway. My husband and I had gotten away with recording people for four years in over a dozen cities. I'd have to be a fool to think our crimes wouldn't catch up with us eventually. I just regretted the timing of it all. We were set to leave this city the very next afternoon. We would have escaped the law once again. That was what made this particularly hard to swallow.

The cops kept us cuffed while we put on our clothes. The Puss & Boots customers all stood around in shock as we were walked out the door of what had become like a second home. It wasn't the ending I had planned. But then again, who ever had a plan for getting caught?

## Lyssa & Jacob

It didn't take long for Jacob and me to get paid on our lawsuit against Danielle and Stewart. They copped a plea to avoid jail time and settled with all their victims. Jake and I were awarded half a million dollars in damages. We used the money to start a production company to produce porn for our online version of Puss & Boots. We used Danielle and Stewart's room to shoot in. It was perfect—it already had the proper decor and it was already wired.

All of our participants were consenting. They signed releases and got paid for their work. We put the videos on our website. Members could access them for free and nonmembers on a pay-per-view basis. It was brilliant.

Alexandria ended up dropping out of school. Her heart wasn't in pediatrics. After much thought and careful consideration, we let her start working the door at the club. Jake and I never did anything there so it wouldn't be like we'd have to hide, and working the door meant she was separated from all the X-rated things that went on inside.

Kelsey was promoted to general manager. She also let Morgan stay with her as a favor to me. I paid her share of the rent and utilities, and whenever I visited Kelsey I got to have a little fun. Jacob didn't know. I planned to tell him at some point. The time just hadn't presented itself yet. And until it did, Morgan was my guilty pleasure. She made me happy. And me being happy was good for everybody. I was a better wife and lover to Jake and a focused, easygoing businesswoman. Everybody won.

*Throw it up, throw it up, watch it all fall out . . .* my ringtone sounded. I grabbed my cell off my desk. "Hello?"

"I think our secret has been discovered," Kelsey said.

"What happened?"

"I see your husband's car parked outside my apartment."

"Oh boy," I sighed. "How did he find out?"

"I don't know. You think he saw her at the Valentine's Day party?"

"She left before he got there."

"You want me to just go in and see what's happening?"

"Yes," I told her, waiting on the other end of the phone as she walked inside her apartment building. I could hear her footsteps come to an abrupt halt. "What happened? Why did you stop walking?"

She whispered, "They're standing outside my door talking. It looks like he's on his way out."

"Can they see you?"

"No, I'm hiding behind the wall."

"Okay, good," I said, then I heard voices. "What are they saying?"

"I'm going to put you on speakerphone, so don't say anything or they'll hear you."

I kept quiet and listened intently to the conversation my husband was having with our former live-in.

"What are you doing?" he asked. "Why did you tell her there was never a baby?"

I pressed my ear against the phone harder. Did I just hear what I thought I heard?

Then Morgan's voice answered: "That's the only way I could see her letting me back in. You know she's spiteful. And besides, had I told her I decided to go through with an abortion she would have talked it over with you—and seeing how you haven't been answering my calls, something told me you would have shot it down."

"So did you?" Jake asked.

"Did I what?"

"Get rid of it."

"Not yet, but there's still time. Are you going to give me what you promised?"

I waited to hear what the promise was, but no words were spoken. Just silence. I whispered to get Kelsey's attention, hoping it wouldn't blow my cover. "Psssss . . ."

"Hello?" Kelsey whispered.

"What are they saying? I can't hear them anymore."

"Nothing. Jake is just looking at her. He seems pissed."

"Okay, put me back on speakerphone," I instructed, right on time.

"You did this on purpose, didn't you?" Jake accused.

"You know, Jake, I wish we had time to lay all our cards out on the table, but Kelsey will be here any minute."

There was that silence again, but instead of asking Kelsey for another visual, I was patient.

"Schedule the appointment. When it's done and I see some sort of proof, I'll make the deposit," Jake said with disgust. "After that, I don't want to see your gold-digging ass ever again. Not here, not at the club, and not at my fucking house."

Suddenly Kelsey's voice returned with urgency: "He's leaving," she whispered. "Do you want me to stop him?"

I thought about it, and while I would have loved for Kelsey to run up on them and bust them with me on the phone, that wouldn't be smart. All Jake would have done was offer some lame justification. I had a better idea.

"No," I told Kelsey. "But as soon as he's out of sight, put me on with Morgan."

"Okay," she obliged.

Then we both waited once again, and I was left to my thoughts. So my daughter was right: there was something extra between Jake and Morgan. But why? I didn't understand how a man who was already having his cake and eating it too would still feel the need to cheat. It was mind-boggling and real damn heartbreaking. Maybe what Jake's doctor had said was real—I recalled an office visit where his doctor had said he was exhibiting symptoms of a midlife crisis. He said it was a real condition with real effects. I admit, I wrote it off. But maybe he was right. Maybe Jake was desperate to feel young again, and with Morgan stroking his ego every chance she got, it was easy for him to get caught up in the fantasy of having a young girl be so attracted to him. But now, I think he had realized it was all bullshit; with his nose finally out of her ass, he could smell it.

Kelsey's voice brought me back to the moment: "He's gone." I heard her footsteps start up again. Then her voice. "Wait, don't close it."

"Kelsey?" Morgan said in a high pitch. "Oh my God, you scared me. I was just looking out the door for you."

"Lyssa wants to speak to you," Kelsey replied.

"Hi, Lyssa," Morgan said into the phone, surprise in her voice.

I decided to do like Kelsey and cut to the chase: "How much is he paying you?"

"Excuse me?"

"I just listened to your conversation with my husband. I know he agreed to give you some money if you get rid of the baby you're carrying."

"Lyssa . . ." Morgan began.

"The bullshit, Morgan, cut it. I'll pay you double to keep it. Show up eight, nine months later and sue him for child support. That's what you really wanted, right? Steady income. Stability. Is that why you didn't go through with it when he put you up in the hotel? You didn't want the lump sum. You wanted the residuals, didn't you? Well, I'm giving you the chance to have both.

This way you can live off the lump sum until the baby is born, and then you'll get your stability."

"I don't understand," Morgan said. "What would you be getting out of the deal?"

"You said it yourself: I'm spiteful. Well . . . I want Jake to pay for going behind my back and getting you pregnant. And the only way I can see that happening is if he has to pay you every month for the next eighteen years of his life. That's why he wants you to get rid of it—so he can shortchange you. But you're a smart girl. You know that lump sums dwindle quicker than anyone ever anticipates, and that a monthly check is where real stability lies."

"I'm sorry, Lyssa," Morgan said with a sob. "I really am. But it's so uncertain working as a live-in. I don't have a college degree. And even if I did, last I checked, college graduates are competing for jobs at Walmart these days. Where I come from, girls have babies by wealthy men to get by. I'm just trying to survive."

I acted like I was sympathetic but she had to be a fool to think I was. And lucky for me, she *was* a fool. "Well, I'm giving you a shot at survival."

"You have a deal," she quickly responded.

"Good. I'll see you tomorrow," I told her.

Kelsey got back on the phone and I said I would talk to her about everything later. I was in no mood to do it right then. She respected my wishes and we hung up.

I put my phone on my desk, sat back in my chair, and thought. I put myself back in my living room with Morgan and Jacob and replayed in my mind the two of them denying having done anything without my consent. The whole time they had both known the truth and had hidden it from me with apparently no remorse. That was dirty. And I felt myself getting emotional. I had to wipe a tear that I felt welling in the corner of my eye. There was no way I was going to cry. I had made my bed and let another woman lie in it. I couldn't help but feel like part of this was my fault.

On the other hand, Jake, Morgan, and I had an agreement. And I may have played a role in breaking it, but only after the two of them had already thrown it away.

Well, I had something for both of them: after Morgan's term and a DNA test proved Jake to be the father, I would convince him to fight her for full custody. He'd take the bait—anything to avoid child-support payments. And as soon as he walked away with a winning judgment, I would file for divorce. Jake would be stuck taking care of a newborn all by himself and Morgan wouldn't get a dime in support. And that would teach both of them a lesson about fucking with me.

## Tori & Kevin

Kevin and I were on the deck barbecuing, welcoming the first day of spring. He was taking the chicken breasts and vegetables off the grill. I was setting the table. We had timed dinner so that we could eat while watching the sunset.

It was Warm Wednesday and I'm not referring to the weather. Kevin and I had given each day of the week a pet name. And we'd spend that day doing something relative to its name. It was something we'd incorporated into our marriage ever since the tragedy over a month earlier.

On Movie Monday, we would go on a movie date or find something on On Demand to cuddle up to. Togetherness Tuesdays were dedicated to quality time with each other. And on Warm Wednesdays we did something romantic, wholesome, warm.

We found that purposely creating our lives was the best way to move forward individually and collectively. We learned that when you intend your life and will into existence what you want each day to be like, it will manifest itself in that way.

We ate our dinner and gazed at the sun as it dipped beneath the horizon. We appreciated the calmness, the peacefulness. We appreciated life. And we were over the moon about the one that was growing inside me. We appreciated each other more too. Or at least I know I appreciated Kevin more. It sounded crazy whenever I thought about it, but somehow going through that horrific ordeal had made our bond stronger. That and the fact that we were finally starting the family Kevin had always wanted.

We were clearing the table, taking everything from outside in. The news was airing on the flatscreen that hung above our fireplace. We never really watched the news, but we weren't going to stop what we were doing to change the channel. In the midst of putting plates in the dishwasher and food in plastic containers, we both heard something that did make us stop in our tracks.

*"Police have discovered the body of a man thought to have fled after hiring a hit man to kill his wife, former supermodel Judith Paxon-Ribeiro. Ferrari Ribeiro's body was found in a landfill in South Carolina. An autopsy report showed he had died of strangulation—the same way his wife was killed just over a month ago. While Judith's family, friends, and supporters view this discovery as a bit of poetic justice, police are diligently searching for Ribeiro's killer . . ."*

The sound of a plate crashing to the floor startled Kevin. He looked at me. My hands were shaking, frantically. He gently approached, lowering my hands. He wrapped his arms around me.

"Just keep to our story," he said in a solemn tone. "Act normal at all times. Don't ever confess to anybody, no matter what."

"And remember," I looked up at him, "we're in this thing together."

Another allegiance was formed, this time with more than our words and our hearts—with our very lives. We both knew clearly what we had gotten ourselves into. The only thing up for questioning now was how we were going to get ourselves out. And despite our efforts to remain calm, this was a chilling spot to be in. The spring had just gone cold.


The End

# ALSO AVAILABLE FROM INFAMOUS BOOKS

## *H.N.I.C.*
### BY **ALBERT "PRODIGY" JOHNSON**
### WITH **STEVEN SAVILE**

128 PAGES, HARDCOVER $19.95, TRADE PAPER, $11.95, E-BOOK, $4.99

*Prodigy, from the legendary hip-hop group Mobb Deep, launches Akashic's Infamous Books imprint with a story of loyalty, vengeance, and greed.*

"The work is a breath of fresh air from lengthy, trying-too-hard-to-shock street lit and is an excellent choice for all metropolitan collections."
—*Library Journal* **(Starred Review and Pick of the Month)**

## *THE WHITE HOUSE*
### BY **JaQUAVIS COLEMAN**

112 PAGES, HARDCOVER $19.95, TRADE PAPER, $11.95, E-BOOK, $4.99

*One house . . . one robbery . . . one mistake . . . Sexual intrigue and violence intermingle in this tense urban thriller.*

JaQuavis Coleman is the *New York Times* best-selling author of Dopeman's Trilogy.

## *BLACK LOTUS*
### BY **K'WAN**

160 PAGES, HARDCOVER $19.95, TRADE PAPER, $11.95, E-BOOK, $4.99

*Finding the Black Lotus murderer is Detective Wolf's chance to avoid an Internal Affairs investigation. That's when things get personal.*

"One of hip-hop fiction's hottest authors." —*King*

---

These books are available at local bookstores. They can also be purchased online through www.akashicbooks.com. To order by mail send a check or money order to: **AKASHIC BOOKS** PO Box 1456, New York, NY 10009
www.akashicbooks.com, info@akashicbooks.com
(Prices include shipping. Outside the US, add $12 to each book ordered.)